Books and stories by William M. Brandon III
The Exile The Matriarch & The Flood
Welcome to Spring Street
The Atheist and The Rapture Button
The Atlantic

visit agentofdiscord.com

Kind words about SILENCE *&* "Selene":

"Hello again, Dean O'Leary, you old romantic in your pinstripe suits and dive bars, barreling through time, looking for respite from this cruel world. In this steel-edged noir novella, William M. Brandon III takes us on a thrilling ride as his anti-hero tries to get to the bottom of things: Can time redeem us? Can friendship? Can love? Silence redux is a pure and dark delight."

— **Saskia Vogel,** author of *Permission*

"Many a yarn has been woven around the quest for love. But that familiar tale starts to fray at the edges when young Dean O'Leary, a bank robber whose pinstripe suit is a better fit than the age in which he lives, packs up his cigarettes and his battered heart to start fresh in Las Vegas. With a voice and style that drag you in, Brandon sets up a character whose neurotic, mile-a-minute mind echoes the desire, anxiety, depression, and insanity found at every intersection on the road to love. From Dean's ultimate highs to his rock-bottom lows (making a quick pit-stop at the surreal), Brandon will take you on an emotional walk in a desperate man's wing-tip shoes—and you'll be hooked from the very first step."

— **Elise Portale,** Editor

"A twisty, topsy-turvy ride with bad people making bad decisions."

— **Jim Ruland,** author of *Make It Stop*

"What one may state confidently without taking anything away from the readers, and I do trust this novella will undoubtedly find readers, is that this is a perfectly captured tale of trapped characters, trapped by their cages whose bars are just beyond their view and out of reach of their chisels. They didn't ask for this and have no choice but to play it out to the end. And what an end it is, and what a middle, and the novella as a whole, a breathless experience."

— **Nick Voro,** author of *Conversational Therapy: Stories and Plays*

"Brandon's style of writing in this novella is timeless. He perfectly captures the humanity of O'Leary. Every puff of smoke, sip of gin, and philosophical rambling has you questioning your life—your wants, needs, and goals. Like O'Leary, we find ourselves wondering: if we reach that one last goal, will we be happy? But money is just a Band-Aid on a bleeding vein, and Brandon shows us that love, true, intoxicating love is what we really crave. Silence is so much more than a tale of romance and robbery. I recommend you give it a read; it may just open your eyes to the world around you, and give you some introspective thoughts on your life choices."

— **Amanda Moses,** *Spring Creek Sun*

SILENCE
& Selene

William M. Brandon III

SPACEBOY BOOKS

Denver, Colorado

Published in the United States by:
Spaceboy Books LLC
1627 Vine Street
Denver, CO 80206
www.readspaceboy.com

First printed April 2023
ISBN: 978-1-951393-19-9

for
William Jr.
Rachel
Shirley

Send William a postcard or letter,
he always writes back
P.O. Box 325
Athens, GA 30603

With Very Special Thanks to...

The Wife and Kids—the Home Team, the Crew, the only three humans I'd spend a global pandemic in close quarters with.

This story has a story...

This is not the book that was published in 2000. This is not the book that was published in 2014. It stands on its own as a subtle remix and the closing of a decades-long journey. When I caught a talking head reporting the death of William S. Burroughs, I was digging through the sofa cushions for spare change. The hardened criminal, always in a proper suit, compelled me to read *Naked Lunch* in 1996. The fractured collection of *routines* felt less cohesive than my photocopy-zine of rants, so I set out to write a novel.

In 2000, a friend offered to publish SILENCE if I agreed to pay for half of the print run. Chaotic would be too kind a description for what I sent him, but for the first time I collected the disparate parts and tried to make them a whole.

While we lived in Athens, Georgia, Black Hill Press published SILENCE as a novella. After working with Elise Portale, I was finally able to see the book as a reader. Fourteen years later, the stories began to have dimension and weight, and it felt closer to completion. Black Hill Press invited authors to contribute to an anthology with *continuations* of the theme or plot from their novellas. "Selene" allowed me to take the story in an unexpected direction.

Nate Ragolia and Shaunn Grulkowski were both published by Black Hill Press during my time as the managing editor. They later went on to manifest the universe-saving alliance known to us as Spaceboy. When Black Hill Press left the publishing business, Spaceboy offered to release new editions by Black Hill Press alumni, Pam Jones, Pepper Chambers, Jordan Rothacker, and Nate Ragolia (himself).

I'm thankful for the opportunity to publish *SILENCE* and "Selene" together; it feels like a chance to offer the complete thought to you. It started out fractured, but eventually took a form; it was refined over time, but still needed a finishing act. Now, I can offer this world to you, in its entirety.

SILENCE

Severing Ties

It was a dry, bright day in Los Angeles and the intersection of Sunset and Vine was dense with movement.

The threat of imminent Y2K extinction had dampened America's feeling of invincibility. The movement of the moment had the inhabitants of Los Angeles dressing down to look like the residents of Seattle, but no matter how you pitched it to the marketing team, Los Angeles was no place for flannel shirts and knit caps. Watching Los Angelinos trudge through their sun-beaten streets wearing enough wool to ward off a Pacific Northwest squall never ceased to amuse me.

A patrol car turned right onto Vine from Leland Way and moved slowly through the intersection. The officers were primarily concerned with the length of skirts on that warm afternoon and were unimpressed by a man in a pinstripe suit standing outside of a bank. They were driving far too casually to be responding to a bank alarm, so when they veered left at Hollywood Boulevard, I returned to watching the street.

Five seconds. They should have already wrapped this up. I wonder if...

Gunshot.

This is it. I stepped inside the bank to witness the boys mowing down everyone in sight. Rich crimson arcs painted the walls and teller windows, bodies lay in broken heaps across the long marble foyer, gunsmoke burned the air. I stepped back outside and cocked my 9mm. I am the point man. I see all things at all times. This was my part in the insidious plan.

That day, everything went horribly wrong. The boys made a pact before we started pulling gigs together that if one civilian got shot, every civilian died. Once someone got capped, it was no longer just a bank robbery; it became murder one. There could be no witnesses. The pact had always struck me as a tough guy posture...now, I know better. Stretch was approaching in the car, right on time.

"Let's GO. GO, GO, GO!"

"What happened; what caused all the chaos?" I looked around the speeding car.

"Some John Wayne motherfucker went for the alarm, so I dealt with him. What was I supposed to do? If it's between us going to prison and some worthless rent-a-cop getting waxed, I say 'bon voyage, Tubby.'" Mike's finger rested on the trigger because he was dying for a reason to squeeze.

Jake was our efficient and unstable head honcho. "Shut the fuck up. We're not in the clear yet, so sit back and try to look like the rest of the zombies in this city. Got it?"

We blasted down Sunset Boulevard to UCLA and ditched the getaway car in parking structure seven. We continued from there in four different vehicles— north, south, east, and west. I traveled south on the 405 Freeway in my black and beaten 51' Mercury. I must have smoked an entire pack of Pall Malls on the way to Costa Mesa.

The world was spinning, and a sudden realization struck me: I was responsible for the deaths of a dozen innocent people. I was barely old enough to drink and I had already stolen millions. I doubted the money would compensate for the guilt. The dead slap of limp bodies against the bank floor and the ping of ricocheting bullets drove all other sounds from my mind. I loosened my necktie in hopes that this oppression would subside—my pinstripe suit was a felonious prophecy.

The 405 started backing up around Long Beach, so I slipped down to PCH to hug the coastline. This was my third gig with the boys, and I wondered when it would be enough. We were already set for life, but our profession became an addiction to the rush. Money is the most important thing in the world. People will die to protect it, and we got our kicks punching holes in their fortified walls. But my blood was beginning to thin. I was losing my edge. I needed to pack it up and head out to Vegas where I belong. What if we were all thinking the same damn thing, but none of us had the guts to say it?

Exactly three weeks later, I strutted into the Knight at the brazen hour of 3 p.m. with a fresh shave, fresh haircut, and a new suit. The boys were seated at our booth in the back. Our trademark cloud of cigarette and cigar smoke obscured my view of Mike, Jake, and Stretch. The cramped, sodden walls and carpeting yawned apathy and none of the lost souls hugging the rail turned from their drinks. I walked up to the bar, gave Tony the Barkeep a firm handshake, and ordered a beer.

"Where ya been Dean-o?" Tony's haphazard beach-bum ponytail whipped as he turned.

"You know, here and there. It's good to see you, Tony. So, what do you charge for a beer these days?"

"It's on the house, Dean-o. It's good to have the boys back in the old dive. You hear about the hoods that robbed that piggy bank in L.A.?" Tony gestured to the television hanging over the end of the bar. News of the robbery was still being replayed on the midday programs when the news cycle was slow. "Got away with a few million, scot-free. Lucky fucks."

"On the house you say? Make that a martini. Wait, make that a double."

"You're a real bastard, Dean." Tony smiled.

"That's what I hear, Tony."

I joined the boys at the booth, exchanged how-do-you-dos, and had a seat.

"What's shakin', Dean?" Mike looked me up and down.

"Not much. Layin' low."

Mike knew something was up; I needed to relax and stop thinking about all of those dead people. It made me nervous that I knew next to nothing about Mike—especially since he outed himself as trigger-happy. He came in on Jake's say-so. I trusted Jake; we busted a few noses together as bouncers in Hollywood several years back. It was all Jake's idea: the robberies, the crews, the targets. He had ten years on me and had done some time at San Quentin. He said he knew people, and I believed him. I brought Stretch into the crew. His daddy grew up in Marion County, Alabama, just 103 miles from Birmingham. Driving fast was what Stretch was born to do.

We sat around and had a bullshit session for about an hour, Mike seemed to relax a bit, then Jake rapped his knuckles on the table to commence the meeting.

"Hey, let's get down to business. Everyone's cut is settled. Dean, yours is in a locker at LAX—here's the key and number. Mike, yours is in a post office box in Santa Ana—here's the key and number. Stretch, yours is in a locker at Ports O'Call in San Pedro—here's the key and number. Gentlemen, job well done. Sources say the police have no leads, except eyewitness accounts that four men in pinstripe suits and black masks sped away in a beaten up Cadillac. Lucky for us, every idiot Ska fan in Orange County owns a pinstripe suit."

"No descriptions?"

"Just one. 5'10" to 6'0", dark hair, sketchy looking skinny kid up to no good." Jake laughed and slapped me on the back.

"That sounds about right." Stretch chimed in.

"No descriptions, good." As the point man, I don't wear a mask. Looks a little suspicious standing outside a bank. If anyone were going to be fingered by a description, it was me.

I finished my drink. "Gentlemen...it's been a lovely evening, but I'm swinging out early."

"Where the hell are you going?"

"Easy, Jake; I'm meeting someone."

"You're a real drag, O'Leary. I'll catch you later. The plan still holds. Keep a low profile for three more weeks. Got that, ya jerks?"

I stumbled to my Mercury and disappeared into the coastal mist.

I watched the sea from the Point Fermin cliffs for an hour before I gave up on Helena. Once again, I sat waiting, holding vigil for someone who let me down. I stretched out on the barrier wall and watched the stars struggle to penetrate the city haze with their million-year-old beauty. I remembered how clearly you could see the stars on the road to Las Vegas. I thought about my absent lady friend and the night we discussed distant galaxies, enveloped in the warmth of a blazing fire. Helena was so alive, so desirable. When she was in my arms, I felt I could convince her to leave her man and run away with me to Vegas, to gaze into the onyx sky and discuss the universe as if it were in the room with us. But I said nothing of what I felt and he was still holding her. If only I could say all the words I desired to, if only my tongue wasn't bound. I would have told her not to beat herself in the head over a decision that is best made by her heart. But I am not that brave, and besides, I couldn't bring someone so lovely into my world.

That night clinched it.

I had nothing left.

The next morning, I put on my black suit, black suspenders, black wingtips, and a fire-engine-red tie from the vault of a 1940's tailor. I was ready for Vegas. I walked to the front door with one suitcase and a black hat, took one final look around my apartment, and left.

Jake was walking up my street and leaned on the hood of my car.

"Was comin' by to see how you were holding up. You seemed pretty edgy last night—even for you. Where ya headed, Dean-o?"

"Vegas."

"How long will you be gone?"

"I don't know, probably forever."

"What will the boys do without their point man?"

"I'm through Jake. That last gig in L.A. gave me the creeps, and I'm pulling out. I've got enough dough to cruise for the rest of my life, or drink myself into oblivion, whichever comes first."

"It pains me to see you go. I thought I'd always have the Deanster covering for me, but if it's what you have to do... How about havin' a beer with me before you jet?"

"Anything for you, Jake."

As was always the case, we ended up at the Knight. The density of sorrow trapped behind the Knight's heavy back door was greatest during daylight hours— much darker in spite of sad strands of sunlight wresting through old windows whose black overcoat had chipped.

"I can't believe you're taking off." Jake broke a long silence.

"Sure you can. You know I lose when I gamble. Always have."

"You gambled on me." Jake responded.

"More like you gambled on me." I reminded him.

Jake thought I was a chump at first glance: skinny, never had a broken nose, did my job without much talking. One night while working together in Hollywood, I carded an aging rockstar's date. She didn't have an ID, so I refused to let her in. The situation escalated into a shouting match. When the rockstar's bodyguard took a swing at me, I moved easily and broke his nose. When the rest of the entourage circled around me, Jake backed my play. The rockstar called off his security detail and they left en masse to patronize another Hollywood hotspot. Jake patted me on the shoulder. *Nice work, kid. Didn't know you had it in 'ya.* Truth was, I didn't; I'd never started a fight, but I had been finishing fights all of my life.

"Besides, Jake, you pitched a solid plan, and with the exception of that last job in L.A., it was always easy money." I had no complaints.

"That's why I picked you. You're a nervous wreck about every single detail, but when it's time to go, your mind shuts off and you react. Look. I need you on this crew. Replacing you will mean rethinking the process. Any chance you'll stay?"

"No chance."

The L.A. gig hadn't shaken Jake loose. I was the only one seeing screaming faces in my peripheral vision.

"When are you going to pull up and call it quits?" I wanted to know.

"Right before my luck runs out." Jake forced a smile.

I never saw Jake again. Gunshot wound to the stomach. Some rent-a-cop tagged him as he was backing out the door with a measly twenty grand on a solo gig. He bled to death on an anonymous sidewalk.

§

110 mph down Interstate 15, Pall Mall in one hand, my lucky silver whiskey flask in the other, and my trusty left knee doing all the steering. It wasn't long before I lost the shirt and drained the flask. I could not wait to feel the 100-percent moisture-free, oppressive desert heat. For some inane reason, there was a traffic jam halfway out of Victorville, so I slipped out to Route 66 and took the nostalgic highway to Barstow. It always made the trip so much more interesting. Deadbeat Barstow evaporated in my rearview mirror and I was finally free of the weekend rush headed for Vegas, our distant desert Gomorrah.

I was parched by the time I reached Baker, but there was no time to stop; I had to keep going. I had just enough gas to reach the Strip and I meant to keep driving until I did. The metal-crested buildings of the Baker Correctional Facility reflected the intense high-desert sunlight as I climbed the hill. The large cluster of one-story, reinforced buildings sat sentry at the gaping maw of Death Valley. The slow crawl out of Baker has knocked scores of cars out of commission over the years; the Baker Grade requires a push and pull of acceleration and patience—overheating a flathead V8 is game over. I patted my dashboard and congratulated my antique car for making the climb.

When I reached the state line, I felt a very intense sense of urgency to start fresh, to begin again. A new chapter for Dean O'Leary. New lives, new adventures, and most of all, more money than I could ever possibly spend. Time to breathe, to write—or at least attempt to. I still clung to a precious few delusions to keep me warm at night.

As I crested the edge of the Vegas valley,
I thought to myself, *you're finally going to be happy.*

Gnawing Cold

Late October, when else does love strike with such potency? The wind is bitter, the Vegas floor is cracked with the pain of brittle cold. The modern sands of The Meadows separate and bleed centuries marred by tasteless decadence and hedonism. Even at the end of the twentieth century, primitive aggressions still inject their venom, and Vegas' neon palaces envelop those who dare tread where addictions run deeper than steel needles under Tangiers' stars.

The desert's chilling nights gnawed at my joints, making me fear life past forty (though I have never thought of life past twenty as anything but the inevitable deterioration of all that is precious—all that is matter). These bitter winds swept my darling Audene across deserts and into my tragedy.

The lethal incision was made in six weeks' time—from my first glance at her beauty until the day I would see her no more. We stood side by side, inhaling carcinogens outside of The Plaza Hotel—she was a vision. Her calm skin glowed beneath her dark subtle eyes, and her delicate nose was peppered with youthful freckles. Her short, mousey brown hair was kept hidden beneath a soft knit cap that covered her head like a big-sister hand-me-down. There was no façade about her, only a brutal and sad truth that she seemed to keep at bay just below the surface. Audene's eyes told of the pain that spontaneous men of ignorance leave in their wake.

I, quite by accident, stepped on her foot and she instinctively delivered a shot to my midriff that sent me stumbling. Such intensity should never have been hidden behind cold, earth-colored eyes.

"Nice shot."

"Fuck off." She never looked up.

"What's your name?"

"Look, I said..."

"Fuck off, yeah, I know." When she lifted her head, I smiled. "I'm Dean."

"Nice to meet you, Dean." She didn't return my smile.

She was like a serpent against an impenetrable barrier. Striking out is the only option and death of opposition is the only acceptable result. We returned to silence, but I couldn't leave it alone.

"Have a nice evening." I crushed the remains of my cigarette against the sole of my shoe and tossed it in a long arc into a nearby advertisement-littered trash bin.

"Audene. My name's Audene." She offered her hand to me; her long fingers wrapped pensively around my hand but seemed to relax and enjoy the warmth of the embrace. She pulled her hand away and tucked it back into her long navy coat as if the entire episode had never happened.

"It's a pleasure. Mind having a drink with me?"

She thought about it for a moment and then relented stoically, "Sure. Why not?"

We left Fremont and ducked into a proper dive on East Stewart.

I opened the door for her, "I come here when the din of slot machines bells becomes too much to endure."

She smiled. She understood.

"I'm glad to see you appreciate Downtown."

"The Strip is Disneyland," she replied quietly.

"Indeed." Well put my fair lady, well put. "What would you like to drink?" The barkeep approached. Judging by his wobbling gait, he'd taken a bullet in a foreign war circa 1950. He stood silently waiting for us to order.

Audene jumped in. "Jameson neat."

Quite an order. "Sapphire and tonic."

The bartender left to pour and Audene lit a long, white cigarette. "You really should watch where you are walking."

I smiled. "Yes, I should. Although, who knows, maybe stepping on your toe was the best mistake I've made in a long time."

She looked at me with playful suspicion. She seemed to be struggling, is this guy for real?

I sat back, investigating. "I'm going to take a stab in the dark and guess that you aren't from Las Vegas."

"Good guess. Then again, is anyone from Vegas?"

The bartender placed our drinks down sloppily and got uncomfortably close to Audene's face and whispered. "If you two are here on a *date*, finish up your drinks and beat it."

"Fuck you, you inbred sister-fucker!" Audene shrieked and threw her neat Irish whiskey in the barkeep's face.

I leapt to my feet, not sure if I should restrain Audene or hit the bartender for whatever he said. I chose the former. I left a fifty on the bar and walked Audene out the back door.

"Hey, are you okay?"

"Yes." She wasn't very convincing. "He thought I was a prostitute."

"Oh." That made more sense. "Oh," it occurred to me a little late: he thought I was the John.

She smiled. "Complete asshole."

I was fascinated by her dismissive strength; we began a long walk amidst Las Vegas's former epicenter. Our journey terminated in the lobby of the Golden Gate Café, where I offered her an early breakfast.

"I should really be going." Her gaze retreated and she began to scan the ground for some sort of escape hatch.

"Of course," I was confused by her desperation to leave. "I'd like to see you again . . ."

"Tomorrow. Same time; I'll take you up on that breakfast offer."

"Perfect." I stepped toward her to offer a parting hug. She swam into my arms and held tightly, as a child holds their totem blanket.

She seemed to realize how tightly she was holding and backed away, looking into my eyes plaintively. She handed me a torn slip of thick ivory typing paper. Its pristine surface marred only by blue ink: her number scribbled madly. Audene turned on her heel and walked away.

I was suspicious—I was afraid for my heart—I was afraid for my life—I was afraid for my mind—but as I watched her glide out of the door, I knew I could not walk away, not now. I watched as she pulled a soft wool cap over her short, chaotic hair. She waved over her shoulder without turning and disappeared into the darkness.

Aside from confusion, I felt the edges of terror. There was something about Audene that I didn't want to know.

The next time I saw her, we ate breakfast at the same spot and she asked me to marry her. I was shocked. She didn't even know my last name. I kissed her for the first time, to amplify the confusion. I simultaneously felt elation beyond my expectations and a fear in the back of my mind. I lost the moment when she kissed me again.

"Yes, I will."

For the very first time, I saw her smile, truly smile. It broke through her storm cloud chagrin, and I saw what I had only hypothesized about—happiness. I brought this woman happiness. I could see it in her eyes, when I touched her, when she laid her head on my chest. Something about me made her complete.

Now, I was petrified. I had said yes to her proposal with an extreme degree of flippancy, but she was dead serious, perhaps as serious as she had ever been in her entire life—but how? How could she be that certain in two days? I felt enormous walls shooting up all around me; I was at the bottom of a cavernous trap looking up at the receding sun. I felt helpless to check the walls and see if they were scalable. This is wrong...this is wrong...this is wrong.

This admission frayed my sense of peace. I was determined to prove that someone loving me as irrationally as Audene did could be enough. I had stumbled on and been slowly bled to death by my own romantic barbs. Chasing again and again a moment that never comes. I will love Audene as she loves me— one day.

Yet, I became more frightened of her frenzy, her compulsiveness, and her obsession with me.

§

"Tell me something no one else knows." Audene looked up at me from her resting position on my chest.

"Hm." There were so many things, most of which would probably never grace my lips again. "I was actually born in this nightmare of a town. Born but not raised."

"Where were you raised?" she asked, rolling onto her side and running languid fingers down my thigh.

"Pick a state."

"Utah." She tried a tough one first.

"Yep. Second through fourth grade. Orem, Provo, and Ogden."

"What? Seriously?"

"My family had a steadfast rule. If a place sucks, get the hell out. Pops never hesitated to pick a new place with cheaper rent and new faces."

"Virginia," she giggled.

"Yes ma'am," I smiled and kissed her forehead. "Your turn."

"No one knows much about me, so take your pick."

"Where are you from, lovely lady?"

"It's embarrassing." She looked away.

"Nonsense, I was born in this nutso town. Hit me with it…"

"Bakersfield. Born and raised." Audene whispered it, like a confession.

"I've driven through. On the way to Vegas, as a matter of fact," I smiled. There was certainly something else to the story, but I wasn't positive that I wanted to press.

"Dean," she sat up on the bed. "I was basically homeless when we met. I came out here to escape Bakersfield, to escape my life and my…"

"Mistakes," I offered.

"Maybe. I love you. Loving me, if you do, probably won't be easy. If it turns out that you don't love me, just…be honest, OK?"

"At all times." Except right now.

§

Whatever she was running from when I found her was gaining on her. Our lazy days of post-nuptial celebration were interrupted abruptly.

"I have to run an errand." Audene stood over me, fully clothed with her bag clutched in both hands. "I'll be back in an hour."

"Um, OK. You have to go right now?"

"Yes." Audene kissed me on the forehead. "I'll be back soon."

It was the first of many errands. My wife began disappearing more often and for longer periods. By the time I had given in to apathy, she would leave abruptly and not return for days at a time. When she did return, she was sullen and eager to lash out. We began communicating only at the top of our lungs. Our pain swelled together and as a result of one another.

When I could no longer accept her excuses, I followed her. I tailed her to the Northside, where she entered a small, decayed neighborhood speckled with grey, near-demolished homes. Wandering humans clogged the sidewalks, and as I sank deeper into the melee, I began to rethink my decision to follow her.

Audene stopped in front of a dreary, two-story apartment building and disappeared into the ground floor. I parked and watched from across the street as Audene knocked on the door for apartment B. A stout, olive-skinned man opened the door and beckoned for her to step inside.

"Kid!" I called out to an adolescent on a bike.

"What?" He was not pleased about being flagged down.

"You live around here?"

"Yeah. Why?" The kid had better things to do.

"I nicked someone's car while I was parking. I want to give them my insurance info. I think he lives in apartment B; short guy, jet black hair . . ."

"Dmitri?"

Perfect, the kid gave him up.

" ...but Dmitri's car isn't parked out here..."

"Thanks, kid." I waved.

Audene emerged twenty minutes later, harried, wide-eyed, and anxious. She looked up and down the sidewalk several times, both ways, as if she were about to cross a highway. She seemed stuck, and could not decide to take the first step; somehow, it was too much for her to bear. She looked about once more in desperation before plopping down on a step and sobbing quietly. When tears ceased streaking her cheeks, she wiped her face, stood, and drove away.

§

Dmitri closed and locked his front door. I'd nearly given up on the bastard leaving his cave. His side window was easy enough to pry open. Dmitri's hovel was sodden with the debris of lethargy: half-consumed fast food, clothing representing various levels of cleanliness, and the reason for Audene's visit —a tiny crystallized mound of meth.

I destroyed the room. I expected to feel rage, but I was consumed by one thought, end this now.

§

I should have seen, I should have *known*. My pensive bride fought a silent war—creating the frame for her agonized portrait. This addiction is the battle without end, a war with no victors.

I walked into our apartment late that evening. I thought she was out, as usual. The apartment was dark, and although I could smell their sweet aroma, all of the candles had also been put out. As I crossed the threshold and hung up my coat and hat, a sense of foreboding came over me. Death was in the room; it caressed the hairs on my neck. Where was she—my pain and my torture?

I felt the wind whip past my face before I heard the crack of my 9mm. I fell backwards to the floor and stared blindly into the darkness. A second bullet pierced my right shoulder. *There she is.* I lunged toward her and wrapped my hands around hers. I gained control of my weapon and stood silent with my arm stretched taunt, the barrel pressed firmly to her forehead. I flipped a nearby switch and saw my broken Audene. I wanted to hold her, forgive her, and let her finish me off bite by bite.

"It is better this way. You don't love me. Set me free...please." She held my hand in place and pushed my index finger against the trigger.

She was dead, slumped over onto the floor. I didn't try to stop her—I was never able to stop her.

§

There's a small silver rock in the desert near Hesperia that I cast my shadow over once every year. I beg forgiveness, severed earth and silence as my witness. This land takes my iniquity and devours it as a child devours mother's milk. No remorse...only hunger.

The End of Reality as
We Know It

I first saw Gaelin in a hole-in-the-wall restaurant on Sahara. The Cuban cuisine was only mediocre, but there was an awe-inspiring painting above booth 13 that very abstractly depicted the Bolshevik Revolution. I loved to sit for hours sipping extraordinary whiskey until the hues swirled together. The paint leapt from the canvas and animated passion and guilt and pain and hope. A young man with chaotic dark hair and thin spectacles was peering over my head at this painting, and I could tell by the look in his eyes that he saw what I did. He felt the magnitude of the artist's emotion.

§

The blistering desert heat had thrust the mercury to a brutal 110°, and our father Sol was punishing me for my decades-late flair for style. It's my fault, but there's something about strutting into a Las Vegas lounge smelling of whiskey and carcinogens, wrapped in a suit your grandfather had tailor-made in 1948, that makes it worth while. I was past the point of inebriation as I lit a Pall Mall and ducked into the Golden Nugget. I suddenly felt like raising a little hell at the wee hour of three o'clock in the afternoon. I wrestled a stool into position and let the cool air, sultry jazz, lack of light, and a frigid glass of gin erase my memory. Some puppet on the television was reporting a story about three chaps in San Diego that pulled off a multi-million-dollar bank heist and disappeared, literally.

"Hello, Jake. Looks like your luck is still holding up," I muttered under my breath.

As soon as the words rolled off my tongue, I heard *Starvation, and not evil, is the parent of modern crime* over my right shoulder. I rose from my position, hunched over yet another blessed glass of gin, to see who in this mindless lounge had quoted Oscar Wilde.

What I saw was supernatural. Soft ebony curls framed her gleaming emerald eyes; looking past these oceans of placid beauty would be a crime against one's self. Her velvet lips quivered slightly, as if she were on the verge of explaining to me everything poignant in this world but couldn't risk that I didn't care. I was absolutely stunned, and for one brief, shining moment, I did care. I needed to know what went on behind the glassy expanse of her jade eyes. This was the type of moment we all wish we could seal in a bottle and cast out to sea, returning endlessly with the tide to remind us that death is a truly tragic end to the lavish experience that is life.

This is where my mistress alcohol rears her jealous head and lashes my tongue until it is subservient and ambiguous. All I could squeak out was, "You're incredible."

This goddess peered into my tortured eyes, tenderly searching for the right words to say. "I'd like to know you, but not like this."

She kissed my cheek and it burned with subtle passion and a very vivid fear that we had simply crossed paths at the wrong time. I destroyed the beauty we should have shared together in the space of sixty seconds. As she slipped away, I turned back to my glass and traced *fuck* in the condensation on the bar.

Three hours flew by and my need to be left alone was intensifying. Solitude and alcohol called to me in unison all too often.

"Make it a screwdriver this time, barkeep." I needed my spirits lifted. The drink came and I lamented letting her go without a fight; my loss of her is a pain I shall always deny.

§

The next time I saw Gaelin, I was playing poker in Caesar's Palace when a hand came to rest on my shoulder.

"Hello, friend." It was the mysterious art lover. I gestured for him to take the seat next to me. I was too drunk to notice that there was already someone sitting there.

"Beat it, pal," were the first words out of my mouth. I assume I said this with conviction because the man picked up his chips and left.

"I'm Dean. Who are you?" My manners tend to diminish when I'm going on my fifth hour of drinking and gambling.

"It's a pleasure to make your acquaintance. I'm Gaelin." His strictly late-'90s attire and prescription spectacles made us an odd pair, but it was Vegas: odd has a higher standard.

"What brings you to this hellhole?" I asked.

"I live here. I've always been a hedonist at heart, and when the rest of my body caught up, I ended up here. What about you? You look like you just rolled out of a Lon Chaney film."

"It's a long involved story of self-loathing, not acceptable for the opening of a friendship. I'll admit, I'm not sure if I should shake your hand or pistol-whip you. I get the feeling there's more to our meeting than simple camaraderie."

"Do you believe in fate?"

"Not even a little bit," I retorted. "I do have a highly developed tendency to walk blindly into dangerous situations. I just haven't decided if you qualify as dangerous."

As a gesture of faith, Gaelin bet $1,000 on the next hand. Cards slid swiftly to land within his gaze. He peered at his hand and gave no sign of victory or defeat. The dealer smiled, as he did at every hand, and arrogantly tapped the rail. He stared at Gaelin, challenging him to keep raising.

As the betting closed, Gaelin laid down his cards.

"Full house, number of the Beast over kings."

The dealer had three aces.

"Well, well, Dean," Gaelin smiled, "fate is apparently on our side. Where to next?"

The Necessity of Adversity I

Jesus, it's cold. Gaelin and I walked out of the casino into the frigid desert night. The Strip lay glowing before us—actually, for me, it was more fuzzy than glowing. Seven hours of drinking and gambling had really put a damper on my sight. I staggered a bit and began falling toward oncoming traffic. In the blink of an eye, Gaelin had his arm around my waist and had restored me to an upright position.

"You're a real bastard when you're drunk, you know that?"

"That's what I hear, that's what I..." I stopped for a moment. Call it my one and only moment of clarity.

"Are you OK? Looks like I'm losing you," Gaelin queried.

"Yeah, I'm fine. I'm just working through some things with my head. We fight a lot, especially when we're drunk."

"Let's grab something to eat. My treat, the last three hands paid exceptionally," Gaelin offered.

At least one of us was accomplishing more than getting drunk. "How much did you make?"

"About ten grand after the last dealer's tip."

"How much did you tip him?"

"A grand."

"You gave that jackass a thousand dollars for doing his job?" I couldn't believe it.

"Trust me, he earned it."

"How do you figure?"

"Let's just say that when you have a reputation as a big tipper, certain things are revealed to you." Gaelin lowered his voice.

"Like what?"

"Nothing concrete, just a change in attitude, or position. A slight change in facial gestures lets you know when to bet big and when to lie low."

"You mean they cheat for you?"

"Not entirely. They're dealing the cards the exact same way, but dealers develop the ability to count cards. They know all of the probabilities; it's their job. So they have instincts like any other gambler, perhaps a little more based in scientific fact, but instincts nonetheless. When sweet cards are swinging around, they'll let me know."

I had completely underestimated Gaelin; I didn't usually make that mistake. "So that full house was a hint?"

"No, that guy's a straight shooter, he doesn't fool around. That's why I smiled like such an asshole as he handed me my chips. He's a tough guy to beat, which is why I suggested we move to another table."

"You're a sly one, all right. So, what sounds good for eats?"

"I don't know, how about—oh shit."

"What's the matter?" I felt the cold barrel of a handgun on my neck. "Oh shit."

We were ushered into a side alley near a service entrance for a casino. I was slammed into a wall face first and a second man held Gaelin at gunpoint.

"Where's your cash, asshole?" grunted the first man.

"What do you mean?" Gaelin asked unconvincingly.

The first man pulled the hammer back. "Don't fuck with me. I have a firearm pressed firmly against your neck. If I sneeze, you lose your head and I find the money on your dead body anyway. It's *your* choice."

I interjected: "Looks like neither of you have a silencer handy. We are approximately fifteen feet away from prying ears, perhaps even a cop. Not to mention about twenty cooks and busboys right inside this door." I rapped on the metal door. "Do you want to walk out of this alley as free men, or do you want to spend the rest of your already quite sad life trying to survive prison riots? It's *your* choice."

I couldn't believe the way I was talking to this hoodlum. I can't dodge bullets any more than the next guy. There was a long pause before the gun struck the back of my head.

Darkness . . .

My head hurt like the night I abused a lethal amount of Goldschläger and ended up in the middle of the desert firing a pistol into the darkness. I sat up and took a look around. Gaelin was on the ground next to me. I checked his pulse. He was alive, but if he felt anything like I did, he'd wish he wasn't. Everything looked dirtier to me for some reason. Almost dying at the hands of amateur thugs puts a tint of filth on the world that one doesn't recognize until they've fallen victim. I slapped Gaelin's face.

"Wake up. They're gone. We must have been unconscious all night—it's 1:00 p.m. already."

"At least we're not dead," Gaelin responded groggily.

"Well, I have ten bucks, do you still want breakfast? Ok, scratch that. Looks like they found my ten bucks." My pockets were empty.

"Don't worry about it—those punks didn't get my money."

"They didn't?"

"Hell, no. The casino cuts a check. I have a tab going at the Golden Gate Café; breakfast is on me."

It was obvious that nothing had changed about the Golden Gate Café in forty years. When something's not broken, don't bother trying to fix it.

Our server arrived, pad in hand and pen poised.

"What can I get for you gentlemen?"

"Steak and eggs, well done," I answered.

"Ditto, make mine rare."

"Say, is Jenny working today?"

"Sorry, I don't know any Jennys." The waitress looked at me, confused.

"She worked yesterday."

"Sorry buddy, I've been here for two years, no Jenny."

Our waitress left.

"That's odd. Jenny served me my usual last night before I hit the casino and ran into you." I was still reeling from our first meeting, the poetic beauty who refused to give me the time of day. I saw her through the windows of the Golden Gate Café, pouring coffee for patrons. I took a seat in the back. When she smiled and said, *Hello again,* I knew she recognized me from my drunken haze in the Golden Nugget.

"As a matter of fact," I reached into the pocket of my jacket and pulled out a piece of paper that read: Give me a call sometime, Jenny—867-5309. "I need to make a quick phone call, man. I'll be right back."

I had a nice shiny quarter in my pocket and the payphone was one of those blasted $1 phones. Wait... $1? When did that happen? I've seen 35 cents, even 65 cents in extreme cases, but never an entire dollar. Ludicrous. I pulled 75 additional cents from my pocket and gave it up; I needed to know what all the confusion was about. The number rang six times...

"Hello?" It was the voice of a man, desperately trying to hide the fact that he had run to the phone.

"Is Jenny home?"

"Who the hell is this?" the man demanded.

"Who the hell is this?" I retaliated.

"I'm her husband..."

I couldn't speak.

"Is this Dean O'Leary?"

Wait, I didn't know Jenny was married, and how the hell did this guy know my name?

"I can tell it's you. You have some gall calling this house, you bastard."

"Now, hold on, mister. I don't know you, and besides knowing my name, I'm positive you don't know me."

"Oh, I know you; you're the scumbag that fucked my wife sixteen years ago and wrecked my family."

"You've got the wrong guy, pal. Jenny gave me this number yesterday."

I was feeling like a person might right before they realize that they have lost their marbles for good.

"The kids have moved out, Jenny and I have been separated for years—she's all yours. I hope it was worth it." He hung up.

This was turning out to be a very strange day.

"Did you find her?" Gaelin dutifully asked when I returned to the booth.

"No, wrong number." I didn't understand what had just taken place and figured hearing it second-hand would be that much more confusing. "Where the hell is our food?"

"I think they had to send someone to Wisconsin to get a fresh cow. I'm going to grab a paper, be right back." Gaelin walked toward the front door.

What the hell was going on—who the hell was that guy on the phone—what the hell was his damage— where the hell was Jenny—how the hell could we have slept together a decade ago—why the hell am I saying hell so much?

A shadow fell over my cup of coffee. Gaelin stood with white knuckles clutching the morning edition of the Las Vegas Journal. I've seen men with guns pressed to their temples, their eyes darting back and forth, waiting to die—I have never seen terror like I saw in Gaelin's eyes.

"I'm positive that I don't want the answer to this question, but what's wrong, Gaelin?"

He couldn't speak.

He dropped the paper in front of me and pointed to the upper right-hand corner.

July1, 2013

Gaelin and I had lost sixteen years in the blink of an eye, sprawled out on cold concrete, traveling through time in a catatonic state. We lost our consciousness and our wallets in 1997 and regained our consciousness in 2013. (Unfortunately, the wallets were still gone.)

"What does this mean?" Gaelin finally broke the silence.

"It means nothing. It means everything. It means that we live in 2013, I don't know." I was feigning calm, more for my benefit than Gaelin's.

"What are we going to do?"

"Well, I don't recall doing anything out of the ordinary that might trigger time travel, so I am assuming that this was not instigated. If we didn't instigate it, then we are probably stuck. We should make ourselves comfortable."

"How can you be so calm about this? We just lost sixteen years. We aren't the same people anymore. We're specters—the real Dean O'Leary is an old man."

"If I survived that long."

"Knock on wood, Dean. If you didn't believe in the supernatural before, you should now."

I rapped the table thrice with my knuckles. Once for Love and twice for Luck.

"I have money stashed all over the Caribbean. I should still be able to access it via passcode. Let's find a place to live and do what we can to come to grips with what's going on."

"OK, but I'm still having a problem dealing with the fact that we're walking around somewhere in this world on the verge of our forties."

I laughed out loud, "We should find ourselves, just for kicks."

"Hell, no. Didn't you see *Back To the Future*, Dean? Even accidentally seeing ourselves on the street could alter reality, as we know it. We may go back to a world ruled by puppy dogs." Gaelin smiled broadly.

"I'd venture a guess that we are not existing in two planes of reality simultaneously. It's more likely you are a wild and particularly detailed hallucination. I've got a pretty strong feeling that this is our new home. This is the hand we've been dealt, let's play...to win."

Las Vegas was no longer a dense cluster of activity in the center of the valley. The City's tendrils reached to every cardinal point and pushed tensely against the surrounding hills and mountains. Vegas had burst and spread, infecting every sun-tortured inch of sand and devouring once-far-off mini-cities to the north and south. The economic boom had saturated the valley with cheap, brand-new homes. Development went wild until it all came crashing down in 2008. Gaelin and I took care of the shelter issue by finding a stranded ironworker from Kentucky who was willing to let his six-year-old home go for a song.

As soon as the deal was signed I went stir-crazy. On a particularly grey Thursday afternoon, instead of turning left onto Las Vegas Boulevard when leaving Caesar's, I swept down to Flamingo, hit 15 going south and never stopped.

I reached Hesperia at twilight.

The small silver rock marking Audene's resting place was gone. I knew the location by sight and knelt under the rapidly waning sun. I had hoped for this small sign of the familiar. Hoped may be a little understated. As the sun retreated behind the mountains to set on L.A., the long shadows began to blur the desert's stark lines. Nothing looked the same; nothing felt the same. I was free of Audene now. In this time, I was given another chance.

I sent a postcard to Gaelin from Victorville.

Gaelin,

On my way to Los Angeles by way of Hesperia.

Sorry for the abruptness of my departure.
I will be back.

As ever,
Dean

I followed a long train of revelers down Hollywood Boulevard. Someone had really done a number on the intersection of Hollywood and Vine. An immense, unseemly apartment complex attached to a vapid boutique hotel consumed the southeast block. Restaurants and bars you wouldn't expect to see until you crossed Highland had become the norm and the old crack-addict intersection was once again a bleeding altar to commerce.

The Frolic Room, a seedy one-night stand of a bar next to the Pantages Theatre, had survived the neighborhood makeover; some things cannot be killed. The same hand-drawn mural graced the long wall inside the Frolic Room, but now it was encased behind protective plastic sheeting. Things must have gotten rough for a little while. I didn't recognize anyone and it didn't look like anyone recognized me.

I ordered a Sapphire and tonic.

"Hey, when did all that mess across the street go up?"

The bartender rested against the back rail.

"Um, I'd say 2010 or so. But don't quote me on that," he smiled tiredly.

"Did they demolish the Taft Building?"

"The what?"

"The ancient building on the corner where the hotel is."

"Oh, is that what it's called? Huh. Yeah, I think it's still there. Historical site. Probably can't tear it down." —That's exactly what I was counting on.

The bartender flashed the same tired smile and walked the length of the bar looking for anyone in need of a refill. I paid my tab at last call and walked down Vine Street toward Sunset. As long as the foundation of the Taft Building remained intact, I had an emergency source of funds buried beneath the legendary intersection.

Gaelin's phone rang.

"Who is this?" Perturbed.

"Gaelin?" Slurring.

"Dean? Fuck, man, you OK?" Concerned.

"Fine, fine, why not? I had, I mean I think I had too much to drink. Gaelin, I had too much to drink." Dismissive.

"Where are you?" Absent.

"I don't know. I just don't know. I am, I mean I am somewhere. Somewhere, OK? I'm working on it, I'm working. Working." Confused.

"Dean, are you still there? Dean? Good. Are you in Vegas? No?" Gaelin had to hide his laughter as his friend tried to swim through a sea of ethyl to form a sentence. "Sounds like L.A. Do you need me to call someone for you, can you make it back to wherever you're staying?" Compassionate.

"No, no. I'm sorry. I don't know why I called. Gaelin?"

"Yes?"

"I'll be back."

"I believe you, man."

"Good. Night. Good..."

I began writing. On napkins, on second-rate motel stationary, post-its: whatever came to mind. Soon, I had compiled an impressive stack of hand-written scraps of pages. These missives were sodden by scattered thoughts, inner monologues and bits of journal-like reportage. It wasn't much, but I was finally writing. I drove back into the Vegas Valley several weeks later.

"Welcome back." Gaelin greeted me calmly.

"Thanks. Sorry about the..."

"Enough said." He smiled.

Life became what it had to. Neither of us were tethered to 2013, we owed the world around us nothing, and it offered nothing in return. I had come to expect little from the world, and time is only an indication of decay; each day was like the next, neither worse nor better—stasis. No time period is universally worse than another. All of the difference lies in who's written the history book. The downtrodden will paint a painful picture, and the victorious will sing the century's praises.

Gaelin got a job to break up the days and nights while I retreated into silence and gave a half-hearted try at writing again. Gaelin hoped to find friends, or at least modern distractions, but like my pointless typing, neither of us were granted external peace or acceptance. He eventually quit his job and joined me in pissing away day after day. Gaelin and I became inseparable because we had no one else.

§

"Wake up asshole, get dressed. It's time to celebrate." Gaelin struck me repeatedly.

"Whuh? Whuh's going on?" Waking up is traumatic. "What are we celebrating?"

"Your birthday, idiot. Get the hell up, it's almost midnight."

"OK, OK, I'm up. How old am I?" I sincerely wanted to know.

"Two martinis, please. Top shelf," Gaelin addressed the heavily pierced, semi-clad bartender. A decade's worth of collected filth and graffiti consumed every wall from floor to ceiling. The Double Down Saloon was a pungent bouquet of bodily fluids and gallons of beer that had penetrated the concrete floors, forming a foul layer of sediment.

"Well, you're a quarter of a century old Dean, living in the not-so-distant future with a guy you knew previously for about six hours. Bet you didn't fathom that life could take a twist like this." Gaelin raised his highball glass and clinked it against mine.

"Could anyone?" I sarcastically retorted.

"Honestly, Dean, do you ever hope we'll make it back?"

"Back to what? I was staring down the barrel of a short bout of serious personal destruction and a hopefully painless exeunt. No one even knows I'm a criminal in this time, so no...do you?"

"I don't know, part of me does. If, for nothing else, just to feel like a part of the Human Race again." Gaelin stared at the mirror behind the bar. We were trapped men; the bars of our cage were just beyond view.

"We didn't ask for this and we have no choice but to play it out."

Gaelin sat silently. He hadn't successfully detached from 1997 yet. It didn't take me long after returning from L.A. I chose to look at it as someone would look at moving to a nicer neighborhood: you're still you, people are still imbeciles, and the rich still run things. The only difference is that you pay way too much money for rent, on a different patch of dirt than before. Something still plagued my mind: I needed to know what happened to Dean O'Leary. In the event that we accidentally stumbled back into

1997, I'd like to know how to prevent any imminent misfortune.

"Gaelin?"

"Yes?"

"This place sucks."

"Buck up, birthday boy, the night is young."

The barkeep walked over, handed me a Newcastle, and said, "You single?"

"Who's asking?" The bartender was definitely not my type.

"Answer the question, smart guy."

"Yes, very."

"In that case, this is for you, regards of the young lady at the table."

I didn't turn to see who she was.

"Tell her *Thank you very much, this is a first for me, and I am flattered.*"

"Sure pal, whatever." The bartender walked back across the empty bar and relayed the message.

That part was true: no stranger had ever purchased a beer for me and sent it through the bartender. It was coy and flirtatious. My experience with women thus far could be better described as aggressive and cold.

"Aren't you going to go talk to her?" Gaelin prodded.

"No, I'm not good at barroom wit. Besides, she's sitting with someone."

"Don't be an asshole, Dean. The woman's not going to send you a drink and ask if you're single if that's her man."

"Shut up, I'm justifying my fear. Drink up, let's get out of here."

"At least look at her."

The last thing I needed was . . .

"No, thanks. Finish your beer and let's get out of this pit."

"OK, you big baby, let's go. We've got more drinking to do." Gaelin sank the rest of his beer and walked toward the toilet.

The woman was stunning. Her icy eyes would compel completely for centuries. She wore a crisp emerald dress whose lines evoked thoughts of a young Evelyn Ankers. All I wanted was to be moved by someone and to feel that I moved them in return. Nothing unique there.

By looking over my shoulder at this woman, I was struck by a familiar fear. Until then, I had been quite comfortable with the idea that I would grow old alone. But the reality of how alone I truly was had me questioning the wisdom of solitude. The way our eyes met, I knew I could give it all to her and thank her for crushing my heart. I continued to glance over my shoulder and make eye contact. I could lose myself to this woman and that scared me. However, it nauseated me to think I may never see her again.

Her severely cut pin-up bangs lent a note of seriousness to her otherwise long, playful, auburn hair. She deftly collected her tresses and pinned them back—revealing her opulent neck as I casually watched. I rose and made my way over to this mysterious woman. I reached for her hand and I felt myself let go of control. I was consumed; there was no hope for me.

"Thank you, I am flattered beyond words."

"That's what I heard. I'm Selene."

Her voice could murmur pointless words and I would remain rapt.

"I'm Dean."

"Ah, yes, of course you are." She and her companion laughed quietly. He rose and bade us farewell with a sly smile.

I was confused: "What did I miss?"

"We were trying to decide who you looked like. I had you pegged as a substantially more attractive William Burroughs in his twenties. Oso, my friend, said you looked more like the fragile Kerouac type."

"But my name is Dean." I smiled.

"Which means you are neither. You are the self-styled Casanova and adventurer that eluded Kerouac and struck Burroughs as a maniac."

She was becoming frightfully perfect by the sentence, so I played along, "Which is quite an admonishment coming from the Gentleman Junky."

She smiled brightly; we'd plucked one another's intellectual strings and our song was rising to crescendo.

"Be careful, Dean—I'll show you why Anaïs was never far from Henry's mind."

"Be careful, yourself; this time, there's no June to stand between us."

Gaelin exited the bathroom.

"I must leave. Will I see you again?"

"You will, Dean."

She smiled sensuously as I touched my lips to her hand. When I pulled my hand from hers, the pain was undeniable. In this bar, in this time, had I found her? Elation tinted by doubt clouded my smile. I turned so that she wouldn't see.

§

"Good morning, sunshine."

"Fuck you, Gaelin. Why are you waking me up?"

"Because I need to give you your presents."

What could I say? I wanted to sleep so badly, but the man wanted to shower me with gifts, and he was giddy.

"All right, all right, I'm up." I walked into the living room.

"Bad news: I didn't get you anything. That was a lie. I have something potentially world- and Earth-shattering to tell you, but first, the good news: you lost consciousness around 3:00 a.m., and you kept muttering Anaïs, Anaïs, I love you, I NEED YOU." Gaelin barely suppressed laughter.

"Don't mock me."

"I drove back to the Double Down and spoke to the young lady who purchased your Newcastle. She gave me this and said she'd written it for you." Gaelin handed me a small envelope.

"Anaïs...Selene," I corrected myself.

"Can't say. She wouldn't tell me, and she wouldn't give me her number either."

"Why not?"

"She said that the two of you were destined for each other and that she knew you would find her if it took a lifetime. Sounds like she's playing games."

My fingers found a piece of paper deep inside the envelope.

Dearest Mr. H. Miller,

I am caught in the immense jaws of your desire,
I feel myself dissolving, ripping open to your descent.
I feel myself yielding to your dark hunger, my feelings
Smoldering, rising from me like smoke from a black mass.
Take me; take my gifts and my words, and my body

And my cries and my joys and my terror and my abandon.
Take all that you desire.

Take me as if I were something you want to possess,
Inside your body like a fuel. Take me as if I were a food
Needed for daily sustenance. I throw everything into the
Jaws of your desire and hunger. I throw all I have known,
Experienced, and given before now.

Love,
Anaïs

"She is playing a game, Gaelin, and I'm all in." She moved me on so many levels. Her beauty enamored me, I adored her sense of style, I was thrust into ecstatic pleasure by her mystery, and I was in awe of her mind. I was hers.

As I rushed past Gaelin, I called over my shoulder, "You're a good man, Gaelin Gilbraunsen, no matter what your mom says."

I showered and shaved with the ferocity of a hurricane and threw on my best suit.

"I'm going to find her."

"Woah. Just like that? You don't even know where this person lives, Dean."

"Doesn't matter. I'll find her."

"Look man, no offense," Gaelin lit a cigarette, "it just seems like you fall head over heels for every girl that turns your head."

"I don't take offense to that. Anything else?"

"I guess not."

I wandered Las Vegas Boulevard for hours on a hunch. Searching for Selene. Praying for a glimpse of my perceived perfection. Knowing full well that I could not be satisfied until I possessed this woman completely, as she now possessed me. The sun began setting, but my intensity did not wane. Then, out of the corner of my eye, I saw silken legs crossed sensuously beneath a magnificent, knee-length, navy skirt. She was staring directly at me over a steaming cup of tea. I rushed to her side, wrapped my arms around her waist and lifted her out of her chair. She dropped her delicate cup and our lips embraced to the sound of smashing porcelain. The very molecules of the universe stood still and silent in reverence for our lovers' embrace. I was right: this union was perfect, I had no doubts, and I had no questions that were unanswered. Her lips were sweeter than the lover's wine Cleopatra shared with Antony, more permanent than the poison Juliet drew from Romeo's lips, and more perfect than a full moon's light cast on a dark sea. I whispered in her ear, "I never want to be apart from you—be with me until the end."

"Until the very end, yes."

We lost all sense of the world around us. I pulled her into a side corridor of the café and began to cover her body with the caress of my lips and my pleading hands. We pressed against the wall and I dove into her flesh, needing to be deeper, to be closer, to be inside her, to be a part of her. She whined and wrapped a long, sensuous leg around my waist as her hand began unbuttoning my trousers. Selene swayed rhythmically against me and wrapped her arms around my neck. I placed my hands firmly on my obsession's smooth, enticing hips. I felt her clenching, never wanting to let me withdraw. Her fingernails dug passionately into my neck as she begged me not to stop. Her body quivered as she released her grip. We were barely able to breathe as we held each other against gravity's forces.

"Get out of here before I alert the police...perverts." The world came sharply into focus. We giggled like children. I buttoned my trousers and darted with my love on my arm out into the cool evening air. All was perfect, all was right...

Schizophrenia

Days of passion and reckless abandon. Give myself completely or lose my Love forever? Lose my Love completely or give myself forever? Hours of contemplation on her eyes and none on myself. Hours of pining for her scent, for her flesh against mine. It's maddening that she holds this power over me. I'm the one who has all the answers, the one who never skips a beat, the one who has learned to never sell himself out.

She has gripped my very being, ripped it from this broken vessel and surrounded it with warmth, emotion, happiness, and, most of all, love. The most pressing question is why?

SILENCE

She deserves a man who sees only beauty in this vile world. A man who cannot fathom being faithless. A man who has not felt the intricacies of betrayal or its aftermath. She deserves this, yet I can't see past my own fear and let go. I don't deserve her, and one day she will realize this. I will be left with my heart in my hand. Can I keep my tortured head above water long enough to show her how much I love her, or will I drown before we can look each other in the eye?

Questions. Questions. Questions. You can ask me questions for the rest of your life and you'll never find what you're looking for until you look into my eyes. I've felt every pain, every joy, every disappointment, every betrayal. I've heard every spiteful word that could ever pass your lips. I've heard it again and again, and my resilience is gone. It's completely gone. I don't bounce back like I used to. I want to be alone. I want no eyes on me. I want everyone in this world to forget that I exist. Stop judging me, stop questioning me, I'm above that, and so are you. It all fades, it all leaves. People leave, love leaves, health runs, joy is gone. The simple things are gone. They came, ripped my heart out, and walked away. Very slowly with feet that move at the pace of years per step, dragging the ground, making the horrible sound of EXIT.

The sound of the stream is deafening. Who says you can't hear erosion? Your warmth has eroded the ice and stone I've so carefully built around my love. You claw at my defenses to reach inside, to feel connected, truly connected with me. You're saving me. I see forever in your eyes, and for once, I'm not afraid. It breathes fire into my veins. It inspires me. I needed you last night. I needed to caress the flesh that so binds me to this earth, the flesh that addicted me, that trapped me in your arms. I want evenings that don't end despite the inevitable sunrise. I want to conquer your heart, and submit my heart and my will to you.

I'm a good man who has a hard time showing it. Caught up in the nothing can hurt me because I've already been destroyed mentality. Supernova waiting to happen—a bright shining star—in a hurry to burn out.

I'm more in love than I have ever thought possible. She consumes me. Positively consumes me. An improper blink of an eye or furrow of the brow, or pulling away of her lips from mine sends me into convulsions of paranoia. Instantaneous fear that her love will someday wane.

Segue to destruction—the end of a century, the beginning of the end—the beginning of the little one's century, only four years' time and torn asunder—dear Sator, alive and dead in the twentieth century—can the twenty-first be any different?—he enters his twenty-third on the twenty-fourth day of March, he enters his twenty-third—forty-six intertwined.

I've lived my life and now I simply exist. Observing painfully, life around and throughout. It's a free feeling of disassociation. But I have connected with two. One, my eternal lover and one, a love I will never acknowledge. Today has been perfect. My pen chases page after page and my inspiration is seemingly infinite. This is what happens when you ascend and look at the world from distant stars— DETACHMENT—such negative connotations to such perfection. Detach and be free, choose to adhere and lose your chance to choose. Draw close to the human race, and the ignorant masses will destroy your life with obsessions.

Consume—Consume—Destroy—
Must Create—Must Earn—Must Give—Fuck—Sleep—Live—
Communicate
The worst of these: communication.
Disengage now...for your own sake.

DAMNED NONSENSE. Rubbish. I'm so violently ill and disturbed by all the fucking nonsense. The last pages of the book meant to save your soul are nonsense. No intelligent, cohesive thought, nothing to gain, all is lost, time, love, interest, money. I'm frustrated. I feel an abysmal emptiness as I turn the last page, as my eyes peruse the last words. Give me something, please, I beg of you, give me something to cling to, something to identify with, allow me to identify with you. I met a person once who spoke my language. I felt so close; I felt a strange shyness when we spoke, when our gazes met. We knew each other's thoughts and we were united. Now, we are as distant with each other as we are with the rest of humanity. The connection has faded, and I will regret it forever.

—Nonsense. Rubbish—

Can I feel a connection when I am so defended? Why desire a connection at all? What weakness exists in my mind that begs for someone to say Yes, I understand—yes, I love you— the real you—I won't ask anything of you-you are my perfection—I need you.

—Misery loves company. I know she feels the same—

Dean O'Leary
Las Vegas
2013

The Necessity of Adversity II

We were married the next day before the honorable Judge Demois. She smiled and gave us her personal blessing based on the testimony. We glowed. People's faces twisted in jealousy and disgust when they saw how repulsively smitten we were with each other. We spent our days roaming the city drinking fine wine, dining in exquisite restaurants, and making love in public places. It only took one sultry innuendo and we would be caught in a tangled web—(purposely) misplaced hands, and the precious marriage of lips against flesh. Once the game began, we were at war with our environment, the very environment keeping us clothed and polite. Yet, her hand on my wool slacks or my hand slipping slowly to the small of her back as we discussed *The Second Sex* would inevitably result in a thorough check of exits and staff. When the coast was clear, we would repair to a darkened corridor or a locked lavatory, returning with the blissful glistening of lovers' guilt painted playfully on our faces.

We spent our evenings in each other's arms by candlelight, speaking about everything that crossed our minds. We stopped briefly to smoke cigarettes during uninspired searches for sustenance, yet never seemed to quench our thirst for one another's touch. We were all any human could ask for from love. Our nights lasted beyond the rising sun and we did not sleep for fear we may be wasting our last precious moments together.

§

"Dean!"

"What is it, my love?" I was surprised by her sudden calling out.

"What's missing from this picture?"

Selene lay naked before me; nothing was missing, and nothing more was necessary. She held her hand up to me, asking me to stay focused.

"What's missing?"

"Your wedding ring. We forgot rings."

"Yes," she smiled shyly.

After a long discussion about the horrors faced by miners of precious stones and metals, we decided on stainless-steel bands. Perfect, beautiful, and slavery-free.

"Now it's official Mrs. O'Leary, you belong to me in the traditional sense." I smiled.

"I belong to myself—you're just officially the first and last person I want to see every day for the rest of my life."

We did our best to keep polite company over the course of the next few weeks. Selene's friends were very warm and accepting, but neither Selene nor I wanted to be surrounded by other people. Our distracted attention was focused on us, and all else—conversation, company, and setting—melted into the background of our framed portrait of perfection.

Private engagements were much worse. We were a bore to all concerned, and given the opportunity, we would slip out of sight, into a garden, into a master suite, into a deserted kitchen, and set about exploring one another's clothed bodies until we were discovered or the weight of our absence became too great to explain away with cigarette breaks or phone calls. Soon, we were no longer accepted in polite company and the short-lived invitations ceased.

The happiness I had promised myself had finally overwhelmed me and I left my doubts behind.

§

"Damn."

"What's the matter?" My still-blushing bride inquired breathily.

"I should call Gaelin and let him know I'm alive."

I hadn't spoken to Gaelin in at least a month.

"Hello?"

"Gaelin, it's Dean."

"Dean. So you're not dead."

"I am. Dead to the world I knew before, and reborn into the arms of love."

"Wow, that's intense, even for you. Can I take the happy couple to dinner so that I can meet this mysterious woman; Ms. Nin is it?" he asked.

"Mrs. O'Leary."

"You're married? Congratulations, Dean. It's settled, we're having dinner tonight. Be here at 9:00 p.m., I'll take care of the rest."

"We graciously accept."

We met Gaelin at the house. He greeted Selene like a dear old friend and I could tell she wooed him as soon as she spoke.

"Let's get going, I'll drive," Gaelin insisted. "I have a surprise for you, Dean."

We drove up Sahara and stopped in front of an enormous supermarket. "We're here."

"We're eating at a supermarket?" I wanted to know.

"I don't think Gaelin would take us to a supermarket for dinner," Selene defended Gaelin.

"Thank you, Selene," Gaelin kissed her delicate hand. "I barely know you and already I swear that if Dean betrays you, I shall take care of you without blinking an eye."

"Easy there, Casanova," I struck back.

We walked through the grocery store to the meat cutter's stand and Gaelin muttered something in Spanish to the attendant. The attendant motioned for a young man to cover the counter, and asked that we follow. We walked through a series of locked doors and staircases.

We emerged into a large, dimly lit, smoky room.

"I can't believe it."

"What is it?" Selene asked.

"This is the restaurant where Gaelin and I first crossed paths. I thought it was torn down in the mid-2000s."

"The government tore it down. The proprietors were indicted for giving aid and support to a terrorist organization. Namely, the Castro government. The owners' only son went underground and recreated his parents' pride and joy within the walls of this supermarket with the help of fellow Cuban ex-pats also keeping a low profile. The owners still languish in holding cells, ironically, on the very Caribbean island they sought to defend. Booth 13 please, Romario." Gaelin smiled as he said this and gestured to the man who had escorted us through the supermarket.

We sat directly beneath the masterpiece that had served as introduction for Gaelin and I—our unspoken appreciation for the painting comprised our first mutual memory. I felt at home. The love of my life and my only friend, together here and now...I was waiting to push pause on the recording of Time and feel this perfection forevermore.

Gaelin fell in love with Selene immediately. He couldn't get enough of her ideas on El Greco. He ignored me completely. They talked and talked, and after we finished dessert, we had drinks. The whiskey was smooth. My love excused herself from the table and Gaelin anxiously reached for the pocket of his jacket and removed a folded piece of newspaper.

"I couldn't bear it after you disappeared, I had to find out what was supposed to happen to us."

"What do you mean?"

"While you were in Los Angeles, I researched our names. Not surprisingly, I didn't turn up, but I did find a few news articles about Dean O'Leary."

"Great," I added sarcastically. "What the hell did I do? What bit of nastiness would I have become?"

"Be certain you want to know, Dean. If you are, I'll gladly tell you, but if you are not sure...you're happy now, so it almost doesn't matter."

"I need to know."

He handed me the newspaper article.

"You died in 1998. According to this article, three unidentified suspects and a man identified as Dean

O'Leary robbed a Las Vegas bank in 1998. They identified the body as Dean O'Leary, wanted for robbing banks all over California. You were shot through the neck during a high-speed pursuit. The other three got away and were never identified."

"I don't know how to feel about this." Untrue. I felt my mind slipping from me and my concentration receding. I was dead. Shot through the neck. I looked down at my hands; I gripped my empty glass to feel its density. I was still here. I had to be. "Whatever brought us here prolonged my life. I thought this was a curse. Now I can't deny that it was necessary. I met the love of my life, I could never bear missing out on that."

"Here she comes, Dean. Unless you think now is the time to discuss where you came from, I'd put that away." I slid the paper into my coat pocket. I wasn't sure if this was something Selene should ever know. It was her right to know, but a better time would surely present itself.

We made our way from casino to casino, quickly making disgusting amounts of money and spending it just as rapidly. The world seemed to be on its knees begging to give its pleasures to the three of us.

"Caesar's Palace?" Gaelin offered carefully.

"Yes, let's go," I drunkenly agreed.

Gaelin and I stayed away from Caesar's Palace. It was no secret that the place gave us both the creeps after what happened. It was time to stop fearing the past and start living.

We strode into Caesar's like two kings and a queen. We couldn't lose to save our lives, and before we knew it, we had received everything but complimentary heroin from the hotel staff. We were all positioned around a dealer who seemed to be making a fool out of my darling and I, but losing his shirt to Gaelin. Selene and I stopped playing and watched as the dealer and Gaelin faced off poker hand after poker hand. The more I watched this dealer—the way he arrogantly tapped the rail while he waited for players to make a move—the more I felt I knew him from somewhere. I caught Gaelin's gaze and he nodded, this was the dealer we had faced on that fateful evening in 1997.

"How long have you worked here...Ryan?" He looked surprised that I knew his name, but quickly remembered that he was wearing a name badge.

"Oh, about eighteen years, give or take." Even his sincere smile contained a challenge: feeling lucky? I dare you.

"Ever face such a worthy opponent?" I asked, gesturing to Gaelin as he brushed his hair away from his glasses. Gaelin was just nerdy enough to be considered a non-threat and he played it up whenever he could.

"No," the dealer answered, "but I always win in the end."

This was definitely the same guy. His cockiness hadn't waned in seventeen years. A young woman arrived with our three glasses of wine, and after tipping her heavily Gaelin raised his glass, "I propose a toast. To my best friend and his eternal love...if she can stand him that long...may a lifetime of memories be made and may you both be kept safely wrapped in each other's arms." Gaelin slid chips across the table, "Dealer, $1,000 on this next hand. You're about to lose again, and then we must bid thee farewell for greener pastures."

The dealer smirked and passed the cards to Gaelin slowly. Then his face changed, taking a ghostly pallor. He recognized Gaelin.

Gaelin's eyes were wide; his white knuckles clutched his cards as if they were his last faltering evidence of reality. I had only seen Gaelin like this on one other occasion. He couldn't speak.

Gaelin laid his cards down. "Number of the Beast over kings."

As soon as the words rolled off Gaelin's lips the dealer laid his cards down.

"Dealer has three aces." Ryan smiled stoically. He never doubted the outcome.

The light around the dealer began to distort and bend. I looked to my love. She reached out in horror.

"Dean..." she whispered, unable to breathe. I clasped my arms around her shoulders. I felt the invisible hands of Time wrap around my body over and over like roots around a corpse.

"I love you, I will love you for all time..." Our lips met. I knew I would never see her again—pulled from her grasp as the world disappeared.

§

I faced myself. I looked directly into my own eyes.

"Hello, Dean," this person said.

"Where am I?" I asked.

This person was now Ryan, the dealer.

"An interesting question. More importantly, are you comfortable?"

"Is this hell?"

"No, heaven and hell don't exist. And now, neither do you. You have departed from the world of the living and come to me. You are in a dimension of introspect. Continuous, stringent, self examination."

"Sounds like hell to me."

"It can be if you so desire," my host was now Gaelin. "Or this can be eternal rejuvenation and understanding. Humans run about like ants under a magnifying glass their entire lives asking a single question: WHY? We can discover the answers together."

"Why have you ripped me away from my eternal love?"

This person's interpretation of Audene whispered, "That was not my doing, Dean. I simply sweep up the mess, I don't instigate change."

"I don't want knowledge—I want life." I looked away from Audene. It was a cruel tactic.

"Then I will leave you to your hell." the person became Selene and turned on her heel to walk away.

"Wait. Please, don't leave me alone," I begged in dire, desperate frustration. "I almost had everything..." I muttered, defeated.

"You have a lesson to learn, old man." I faced myself again, age eleven. "Adversity makes you act. Without it, decisions don't exist. Without decisions, there are no options. Without options, there is no reason to think."

Age sixteen..."If you do not face adversity, your path is clear and so is your mind. Enjoy the beauty of adversity; let it flow through and around you. Push against it and you will find direction."

Age twenty-five..."Let it push against you and be swept away in aimless frustration."

Death was suddenly distracted.

"Goodbye, Dean."

Goodbye? What did it mean? I started coughing. Bright, white light began flooding into my eyes, awakening my senses. People rushed about in white uniforms, latex gloves, silver badges. Blood from my chest poured through the latex-clad fingers of a young EMT.

Darkness.

"He's back, we've got him. That was close."

I thrashed against the gurney.

"Calm down, you've been shot. We're taking you to an operating room."

The mask on my face began dispensing its invitation from Morpheus.

"Gaelin!" I bellowed, hoping it rose to a shout.

"Your friend is fine. Please, just relax and breathe deeply..."

§

My doctor asked me how I felt.

"Like shit." Every grimace-inducing movement took total effort. "What happened?"

"You were involved in a shooting—I'd stop moving around so much, helps with the pain. The bullet entered your back, hit your left ninth rib and barely missed piercing your lung."

"I don't remember..."

"He shot you in the back, Mr. O'Leary, probably while you laid there unconscious. Get comfortable— you're not going anywhere anytime soon." The doctor turned to leave.

"Where's Gaelin?" I called out.

"Your friend was released. He should be here soon. He comes every day."

§

I woke as Gaelin entered the room.

"Dean, they told me you were awake. How are you?"

"Good, I guess. Didn't die. Still don't feel exactly rooted. Do you?"

"More like uprooted..."

"Good. I don't know what to think about what happened. How am I supposed to..."

"Look Dean, you're going to heal up and be back at the tables in no time. Don't let a couple of thugs ruin your life..."

"Thugs? I wasn't talking about thugs. I was talking about Selene..."

"...what happened to us happens to people all over the world every hour of every day. Who is Selene?"

"Se—" Had I gone mad? "What happened to us?"

"We both got knocked in the head while being robbed—in your case, shot, as well. Did you lose your memory, too, man?" Gaelin laughed uncomfortably.

He didn't remember. Or, more frightening, I had lost my mind.

Gaelin and I parted ways once he felt assured that I was on the road to recovery. With no shared memory of what had happened to us, we were strangers and our inaugural experience as friends had been violent and unpleasant by any person's standards. I couldn't let go of my images of Selene. I refused to believe that it was all an elaborate hallucination. Whether Gaelin remembered or not, he receded into the neon blur and I retreated to North Las Vegas to erase Selene from my mind.

Confrontation

White, wispy smoke wound itself between and around the long strands of midday light that bisected my room. I followed the pillar of smoke to its source, cradled between my fingers. My mornings began the same. Before I could inhale my first deep breath of oxygen, I fumbled for my cigarettes, and with a strike of flint, I was inhaling the perfect ivory smoke spiraling in the sunlight that pierced through my window. This smoke, as transparent and light as it appeared, obscured the sunlight.

I could never again see her...my true love. She was the only beacon of light I had found in this cruel, destructive world. Since losing my darling Selene, I left the house for two reasons and two reasons only:

alcohol and cigarettes. Nothing else mattered to me. Without alcohol, I had no motivation, no drive, no need to better myself or even try. I needed it to function—I had sunk beneath the surface.

I transplanted myself to a small studio apartment on the north side of Las Vegas. The rent and conditions were meager, but I was in no mood to wallow in luxury. I simply needed to achieve a constant state of inebriation, fuck all else. Gunshots rang out all around, day and night, and somehow, I found this comforting. I even decided to join in on the decadence and found great pleasure shooting at the wall in my studio as I lay in bed, drinking the hours away. After three months (and three times as many visits from the police), my wall became a great crater-ridden monument to my angst. I was careful not to shoot out my window, but I shot through the wall on two occasions. It occurred to me at the time that I should fear my bullet finding a target outside of my tiny universe, but that involved caring about something other than myself, and that no longer appealed to me.

Under my solitary window was a small wooden desk with a 1940 Underwood typewriter resting snugly on its surface. Next to my typewriter was a tall, sensuous bottle of whiskey. It was time for breakfast. I stumbled to my desk, barely opening my eyes to the afternoon sun. I stared at the Underwood as I poured a belt. Who was I kidding? I had never been a writer.

Suffering was supposed to feed a writer's creativity, yet I could barely lift a finger to press a key.

I used my index finger, between drags off my cigarette, to type:

d-e-p-r-e-s-s-i-o-n.

I looked out the window, the children didn't play in the street in this neighborhood. My apartment was tiny, dreary. The grey walls of the single room were broken twice, once by a dark doorless closet, once by the black front door. Light was a luxury, one I rather liked denying myself. I rolled over and picked up a copy of *On the Road*. I promised myself that I would read it once a month in hopes that its powers would provoke me to get up and go, to do something...it always had before. I lit another cigarette. Only three left. I'd have to get up and go out soon. After three pages, Kerouac's optimism began to seem sad and naive. I set the book down and stared at the holes in the wall. Why me? Why couldn't I have gone through life not knowing Selene? This sense of loss was too much for me to bear; this depression had taken over, consumed me from within, and slowly, very slowly, eaten away at my very core. One cigarette left; time to get up.

I wiped away a circle in the condensation on the bathroom mirror. In a third-person daze, I ran my hands over months' worth of beard. I looked like a completely different person. I slicked my hair back as I always had—it was an odd combination of disorder and control.

I wanted Selene. I wanted what was; I wanted the future. If I couldn't have it, I preferred to rot away...slowly.

I stepped out into the late afternoon heat. It was one of those rare days in Vegas when the sun was mostly obscured by the clouds. I pulled the collar of my jacket up around my neck, tucked my hands into the pockets, and began the block-long jaunt to Andy's Liquor-Beer-&-Wine-Emporium.

Electronic doors opened to the stylings of the *Stayin' Alive* soundtrack. Andy "D" was the owner of this fine alcohol-dispensing establishment and a movie addict in denial. Andy knew every line, every scene, and every actor or actress from every movie you or anyone else on this spinning globe has ever seen. One sentence of dialogue could evoke title, character, and situation instantaneously. Andy always had a smile on his face, mostly for P.R. reasons, and never showed negativity on the outside.

"Dean, how they hangin'?"

"To the left. Why the hell are you still here? You know I can't steal when you're around."

"Dean, Dean, Dean, always trying to get rid of me."

"Actually, it's good to see you. What's new in the high alcohol content section?"

"I have some serious vino from the Motherland arriving this evening, definitely worth checking out. A little expensive, but since it's you…"

"Andy, my boy, I only drown my sorrows in whiskey."

"Well, I'm sure you know where to find everything. Help yourself. Oh yeah, Dean, we also received a shipment of Bombay Sapphire today."

Gin. It had been a while since gin passed my lips. Reminded me of the good old days.

"Thank you, kind sir. I shall return."

Let's see, six-pack,whiskey, gin…what the hell? It's been too long.

"Ring this up and make it snappy, the alcohol's a-calling me."

"What are you doing to…I mean, with yourself, these days? Are you gainfully employed?"

"Let's just say I'm independently wealthy."

"Why the hell do you live in this part of town?"

"It's a long, sordid tale Andy, and I have drinking to do."

"I'm sorry, Dean. I didn't mean to offend you."

"It's just been an interesting couple of years for me, and I'm a little touchy as a result."

"Are you a poker-playing chap? I've thrown together a Monday-night poker game at the homestead. If you're interested, here's my address. 10:30 p.m. sharp—you know how poker players are: nobody likes a late entry. Bad luck, you know?"

"Thanks. Perhaps I'll stop by."

As I walked back to my building, I noticed an eerie tension in a circle of hoodlums next to my door. I'd seen them around and they seemed harmless, but I saw fear in their eyes that day. I looked up and one of the older boys was blocking my path. He had a switchblade in his right hand and it snapped open revealing a shiny four-inch blade.

"Alright man, here's where you cough up your wallet." Anxiety was dripping from his tongue and the aroma of fear surrounded him like cheap cologne. "I said, give me your fuckin' money."

I stood there silently. He started moving the blade around in his hand.

Petty crimes were enough to get a kid from North Las Vegas permanently in the system. These kids were trapped and they knew that one day they would become trapped men unless they acted. They were testing me. Now they had to know where I stood—the odd man out. They had to know if they owned me through fear. The rest of my stay here depended on my reaction.

"The money I have in my wallet belongs to me. I would appreciate it if you let me pass."

"No chance, old-timer. Hand over the cash, now."

Old-timer? I set my bag on the ground.

"I'm not giving you my wallet. End of story."

I called his bluff, and now he had to react. The boy lunged toward me with the knife. I stepped to my left and caught his wrist. I grabbed him by the back of the neck and slammed him against a wall, hitting his hand against the bricks until he dropped the knife.

"God damn, you're slow. How old are you?"

"Fuck you." His voice strained from his face being pressed against brick.

I tightened my grip on his neck.

"What's your name?"

"Fuck you."

"So, let's talk. You are all invited to listen in," I gestured to the rest of the adolescents that they should gather 'round. "I want to live here without worrying that some punk kid is going to try to off me for the twenty dollars I have in my wallet. Is that too much to ask?"

I tightened my grip on his neck demanding an answer.

No one said a word.

"I'll take that as a yes." I opened my jacket and flashed my sidearm. "Leave me alone and I promise not to pick you off one by one in the streets out of sheer boredom."

None of them spoke. Their pale, blank stares told me that I had either gotten through to them or that they were soiling their pants. I was satisfied with either outcome.

Those dumb-ass kids were brave, but they'd be dead before they saw eighteen.

Do You See Forever In Her Eyes?

I reached out to Gaelin after being buried in my own self-pity for more than a year. We met at the Golden Gate Café.

"Man, you look like shit."

"Thanks, Gaelin. Is it the beard?"

"Sort of. It's more the gaunt face the beard is trying to hide. What's on your mind, Dean?" Gaelin seemed neither pleased nor upset to see me.

"A couple of things. First, I know you and Sarah are planning to leave Las Vegas in the fall. If this woman is what makes the world bearable, then I want this for you."

Gaelin looked confused.

"I followed you."

"Dean."

"I know. Hear me out."

"You're insane…"

"I know you two need a good start and as it turns out I need a new start as well."

Gaelin lowered his head, "Meaning?"

"Meaning a couple of my ex-crewmates ran into trouble in L.A. and one of them sold me out." Jake was dead, so Mike and Stretch went freelance and paid the price. Stretch went down without much of a fight. Mike shot a responding officer, was captured four blocks away, and sat in a holding cell detailing the whole sordid mess. "My accounts are too hot to access. Somehow, they haven't found me yet, but it's only a matter of time."

"What does this have to do with me?"

"One last job. To send you and Sarah off into the world without a care and to make me well again."

"I don't know…"

"It's easy money. Small bank, low traffic. They send for armored trucks every Tuesday. I have a third lined up, he's a pro. I'm driving and watching the door. You just have to stand there looking menacing while our third bleeds the place dry."

"Maybe."

"I trust you. Besides, there's no one else," I added.

I invested no effort in hiding my agenda. I'd been where Gaelin thought he was. In that mystical land of numbness—of love—of proposed and accepted matrimony...head in the clouds...mind locked in silence, unable to affect the outside world.

"You have no reason to trust me, Dean."

"You're wrong. I have my reasons. Do this job with me. A send off and a toast to forever with Sarah." I pulled a cigarette from my pack and tucked it behind my ear. "I'll be back in five—think it over."

I knew how these things panned out: he will wake up one day and realize that the last thirty years of his existence were a lie. This is what Gaelin should be thinking about. Not puppy dogs and picket fences but whether or not he can see forever in Sarah's eyes. If he can't, he must end it. She may still forgive him.

Time destroys indiscriminately. If there exists a doubt in his mind, a weak link in Gaelin's love for Sarah, Time will devour both of them.

"Dean," Gaelin walked out onto the sidewalk. "I'll do it. Contact me about planning."

"Will do, Gaelin." I wanted to ask him..."Hey, what would you do with a glimpse of your future?"

"Change whatever I fucked up. Why?"

"Doesn't matter. I'll be in touch."

§

On the next full moon, I made my way to the back of the bar and used a payphone to call Gaelin.

"It's time."

"See you soon." Gaelin hung up.

I tripped over my feet while flipping a tip onto the bar. I had intended to leave several hours ago. Tempus fugit.

When I arrived at the Peppermill, Gaelin, Sarah, and Anthony—an ex-con from Watts hired for the job—were already getting antsy.

"What's shakin', kids?" I smiled calmly.

"Lookin' sharp, Dean." Anthony was a sweet-talking con-man who took up robbing piggy banks after doing ten years for fraud.

"Thank you, sir. Much appreciated."

"Dean, this is Sarah," Gaelin gestured toward the soft–hued beauty to his right. Her long golden hair washed over her shoulders casually. She lacked the frailty of innocence and seemed a realistic bulwark against Gaelin's weary ennui. Her handshake was firm and her eyes never left mine.

"It's a pleasure, Dean."

"The pleasure is mine, Sarah," I slurred unconsciously.

"Want a drink to steady the nerves?" Anthony offered as he signaled to their cocktail waitress.

"No, I'm steady as they go...come."

"You don't look steady," Sarah added.

"Look again, sister," I shot back.

"This seems like the time to instill confidence in your team." Sarah seemed hell-bent on attacking me. Probably on Gaelin's behalf. What awful things had he told her about me?

"Dean," Gaelin grabbed my arm, "are you drunk?"

"No." Yes.

"You've got to be kidding me. Sarah, we're out of here..." Gaelin stood to leave.

"I'll drive." There was no hint of fear in her voice.

"No way." Gaelin slammed his hands on the table.

"He's right, no way."

"Thank you, Dean." Gaelin sat down.

"It's not a terrible idea. I mean, shit, with you concentrating on the door, everything will go a lot more smoothly, and we can always retrace our steps back to the hotel I set up."

"I can do this." Sarah stared me down.

Gaelin's face twisted—this was a conversation she should be having with him. Instead, she was going toe to toe with me and I couldn't help but smile.

"Fine. Sarah's driving. We good?" I looked at Gaelin; this was his chance to call the whole thing off.

"Good." He relinquished his say on the matter.

"OK, let's go over the timing again. We'll leave here in," I checked my pocket watch, "thirty-three minutes. Anthony will retrieve the car from the parking garage, pick us up from Boulder Station, and we'll head to the target...

"Remember, there is only one entrance. I will be at the door. If someone is going to enter, I'll escort them in and put them under Gaelin's control. Anthony, you know what your job is. Do not stop for anything. Sarah will swing back around in six minutes. None of us can be late."

§

I paused to hold the moment before the storm. To keep it as an island, for refuge, to return to.

"Are you ready?" I asked all around as we pulled to a stop in front of the US Bank on Flamingo.

"Yes," Gaelin answered immediately.

"Oh yeah," Anthony chimed in, smiling.

"You bet," Sarah stared straight ahead and watched the flow of traffic.

"Then, let's go."

The sun scorched my neck. The knot in my stomach was a familiar one. I watched Anthony and Gaelin slide ebony sheathes over their faces and took my place outside the entrance to the bank. I lit a Pall Mall and carefully rolled the end with my tongue. Smooth as silk, drunk or not, I was on point.

There were some obscure people on the streets of Vegas that afternoon. The searing heat brings out stranger folks than Hollywood's full moons can boast. A woman walked directly toward me. Black sunglasses, cheap suit, and unearned arrogance.

I slid submissively to the side, and as I swung the door open for her I pulled my 9mm, cocked it audibly, and pressed the barrel against the small of her back. She did not scream.

I tenderly told her to lay face first on the tile and remain quiet...please. Anthony had already opened and emptied the appropriate drawers and files and was exiting the vault. Gaelin was stone cold and concentrated superbly on every individual in the bank.

"Five seconds," I called out. I stepped back into the intense heat. The streets warbled like asphalt furnaces cooking the air, lending an underwater blur to all things farther than a hundred feet. The steady flow of sun-oppressed passers-by had ceased; Flamingo was dead silent.

Something felt wrong. I couldn't put my finger on it. Maybe it was just the fact that it was 115°. *Here comes Sarah, perfect.* Sarah was turning right off Howard Hughes Parkway. Anthony and Gaelin walked calmly out of the front door while I covered them. She pulled up as we reached the curb, and we stepped into the running vehicle. Gaelin, Sarah, and Anthony started shouting and celebrating.

"Shut up, we're not out yet. Let's try to keep a low profile until we hit the spot," I barked.

"Lighten up, Dean. We pulled it off." Anthony put his hand on my shoulder.

I felt it again. My stomach tensed; something was wrong. Sweet adrenaline flew in the breeze; the sour aroma of anticipation hung around it like a steel cage.

"Everyone put your seatbelts on and ready your sidearm."

"What's up, Dean?" Gaelin asked.

"I don't know, just strap up and be ready for anything."

Sarah looked briefly in the rear view mirror.

Maybe Gaelin was right. Right about Sarah. Maybe she was the complementary soul for his tortured existence. Maybe she could truly, finally make him happy. I hoped it all worked out...

"Dean," Sarah leaned toward me, "I think we're being followed—"

Crimson gushed from Sarah's neck and her life flooded onto my face and hands. Her head slumped against the wheel and her lifeless foot depressed the accelerator. I lunged across the seat and grabbed the wheel to steady the car. Gaelin was frozen in shock.

"Anthony, undo my seatbelt!" I screamed to the back seat.

I unlatched Sarah's restraint.

"Dean, no!" Gaelin reached forward to protect his love; tears streamed down his face. I held him back as he tried to climb into the front seat. I was able to reach the door handle and push Sarah's lifeless body out of the car. She spun, reeling onto the asphalt and under the wheels of our pursuer's car. The car began to skid, slid across the opposing lane of traffic, and ran up and over a nearby parked car—hood-first through the front window of the Lime's Discount Mattress center.

"DEEEEEEEEEEEEAN—You fucking bastard! I'll kill you with my bare hands!" I took control of the car and Gaelin lunged for my throat. Anthony wrestled him down and pinned him as he kicked and thrashed.

"Anthony, keep him down. I'm getting us out of here."

The car chasing us was a brown Crown Victoria, most likely an unmarked detective's car. Must have been on the block when the bank alarm call left dispatch. No one else appeared to be tailing us, least of all marked police cars. Sirens filled the air, but they were all headed to the bank. He must not have had time to call for backup or give a description of the car. It would be a matter of seconds before helicopters were airborne. I cleaned the blood off the windshield with my shirt and collected myself. After all, everyone in Vegas has a bullet hole in their car at one time or another.

I fish tailed into the parking structure of New York, New York and raced to the fourth level. I helped Anthony drag Gaelin out of the backseat. Gaelin, barely able to stand, took several desperate swings and finally connected a fine right hook to my jaw. The pain wasn't physical—I knew he blamed me for Sarah. Gaelin collapsed to the ground sobbing.

"Gaelin, listen to me. We need to move, or we're dead men."

We walked to the hotel entrance joining the fourth floor of the parking structure. Anthony had a suite set up the night before where he was making himself visible with a couple of lady friends. When he opened the door, the ladies were still asleep.

"Perfect, they don't even know you left. Anthony, get undressed and both of you, give me your guns."

Anthony slid between the two prostitutes. Gaelin and I sat silently across from each other in the dining room; I lit a cigarette. Gaelin stared through the large windows surrounding the table. His rage had been overridden by a numb futility.

"Gaelin, I'm sorry. It wasn't my idea to have her drive."

"Fuck you, Dean. This was all your idea. She shouldn't have been driving; she shouldn't have even been there. It was supposed to be you. You were supposed to take that bullet."

He was right. According to the newspaper article, I was supposed to die in that car.

"How do you know that?"

"She was never supposed to be there," he shouted, as if I were too dense to follow along.

The girls stirred.

Gaelin lowered his voice. "This was all for money. The one thing that has never brought either of us a stitch of happiness. Cut me out; I don't want any part of it. It's only a matter of time before they identify Sarah's body and start looking for me. She won't even get a proper burial."

"Gaelin, I think you should stay put for a while," I grabbed his arm.

"The rest of my days will be haunted by the question, *what if?* This is what helplessness feels like—I completely understand you now." He pulled his arm away and slammed the door behind him.

A gorgeous woman barely wrapped in a sheet stood in the foyer...the epitome of a siren. Her tired eyes were dramatically shadowed by black—some strokes by hand, some dedicated to years of late nights and cocaine brunch. Above her scarlet lips and windblown cheeks lay the cold blank stare of an actress searching for her motivation. Her movements were superb—rehearsed. She seemed to have lost her way playing the part—being something to everyone erodes sincerity. I learned the hard way that, in the end, the money can never be spent on happiness, only on controlling the pain.

"Where did you come from?" She asked mechanically.

"Just visiting. You're off duty, feel free to have a seat."

"You're not some kind of *get to know me* John, are you?"

"No. Like I said, you're off the clock," I lit a cigarette for her. "Where are you from?"

"California."

"Where?"

"Why?"

I sat back and took a long drag from my cigarette.

"You don't have to answer. I'm just curious."

"Good."

We sat silently for a long while.

"I'm from Burbank. Born and raised," she recounted stoically. "And I bet I can answer the rest of your questions as well: I came from a good family, no one ever touched me growing up. I realized I could make a lot of money by doing something I did all the time anyway, so here I am. Anything else you want to know?"

"No, that clears everything up."

"You don't want me to pretend that I'm a good girl, just doing this to get through college? To finish my master's degree in chemistry? To feed my bastard kid or afford meth?"

"No. You've made your point," I conceded.

"Keep your pity to yourself, asshole."

I picked up my hat and made my way into the hall. I looked both ways, but Gaelin was really gone.

I walked down the street feeling the weight of the world resting squarely on my shoulders. I slid into the joint I had frequented years ago and sat down to drink myself into oblivion. I laid a $100 bill on the bar and instructed the bartender that it was hers to keep under two conditions:

"Leave me completely alone. When I signal for you, pour me your finest whiskey, and then refer to condition number one."

She accepted, and I brought the glass to my lips. I could smell my salvation in its intoxicating vapors. Heat overtook me as blood rushed to my head, thirsting for and craving the numbing medicine. I tilted the glass, but before I could appease my addiction I saw something in the mirror behind the bar—ebony curls and burning emerald eyes. There she was, my angel with Wilde on her lips.

After Selene, after all that had happened, Jenny walked back into my reality. It could not be blind coincidence, and fate was a bedtime story for infant charlatans and the pounders of pulpits. No, there was no reason for her to interrupt my life, but I would not let her slip by me again. It was time to let go of Selene. It was time to face the fact that she and I were separated by powers outside of our control, and no matter how much I loved her, no matter how much she loved me, we could never reclaim what once was. My memory of her was so vibrant; she was so beautiful, so utterly disgusted with the banality of this universe.

"Goodbye, Selene."

I had to try to love again, or die alone. I could not accept this lying down—I had to try to alter fate, I had to try to control destiny, I had to try to see forever...

Selene
a continuation of SILENCE

"We don't have much to hold her on since the dealer isn't pressing charges. We'll have to cut her loose…"

"Over my dead body," a stern voice boomed from the doorway. Stanley Lankin's stomach had distended and his fierce Stalinist mustache had greyed with time. His casual khaki slacks and cheap button-up shirt made it clear that although he was retired, Stanley would always be a cop.

"Stanley, good to see you." Detective Pinkerton of the Las Vegas Metro Police division shook Stanley Lankin's outstretched hand.

"I got your call about a hit on the O'Leary case. Is this the girl?" Stanley pointed to the sobbing siren seated in the interrogation room. She looked fresh from a brawl at a USO dance.

"Yes, Selene. O'Leary." Pinkerton's eyes narrowed.

Stanley looked ready to jump out of his skin. "Break it down for me."

"Selene was picked up at Caesar's Palace after assaulting a poker dealer. From what we can tell by watching the security tapes, she lost a hand to the dealer and came over the table to extract her pound of flesh. Here's where it gets weird. As she's shaking the dealer, she's screaming, *Where is he? Where is he god damn it, don't make me kill you.* She was gesturing to an empty seat at the table and chanted repeatedly, *He was right there, right there.* So security wrapped her up and while she was in their custody, she begged them to review the casino's security tapes. She claimed that her husband, Dean O'Leary and his friend Gaelin—no last name—were at the table and disappeared."

"Disappeared?"

"Yeah, like a ghost story, or a timewarp or something. Anyway, I remembered that you worked on a case involving a Dean O'Leary for several years..."

"Ten years," Stanley confirmed.

"...ten years. I'm sure the name hit is just a coincidence, but I thought I'd call you anyway. This one is a 5150, she's drunk as hell and has her wires crossed."

"Maybe. Can I talk to her?"

"Stanley, you're retired, I can't let you..."

"Just for a moment. If she knows where he is, I have to know."

"Look, I understand, but it's not going to happen. I can go another round with her and see what she knows about her husband—you're welcome to listen in."

"Fine."

"You're welcome." Detective Pinkerton walked back into the interrogation room and closed the door behind him.

"Selene."

"Did you review the security tape?" Selene's bright blue eyes were clouded with tears and her voice had the shrill undertone of desperation.

"Yes, we've been over that, Selene. We saw the whole thing."

"Then you saw Dean."

"Selene," Detective Pinkerton said, sighing wearily, "we didn't see anything out of the ordinary aside from your attempted murder of the dealer. Ryan, I think is his name."

"Ask him, he knows."

"Ryan didn't have anything to add. He's still pretty shaken up."

"Of course he is. They disappeared."

"Dean?" Pinkerton asked.

"Yes. And Gaelin." Selene placed her head in her hands and began to cry softly. Her disheveled auburn hair fell below her shoulders in long, pooling curls as she shuddered.

"So, you were all out for a night on the town, and decided to play a little poker at Caesar's Palace?"

Selene smoothed her navy blue dress and composed herself. "We were celebrating our nuptials with Dean's best friend."

"Gaelin?" the detective interrupted.

"Yes. We met at Gaelin's house."

"Had you met Gaelin before?"

"Just once. On the night I met Dean."

"Okay. Where did you meet Dean?"

"At the Double-Down Saloon. I bought him a drink." Selene smiled for the first time. "He was too shy to talk to me, but Gaelin returned later to make sure we saw one another again."

"Nice friend."

"Without question."

"Then?"

"Then Dean found me. He wandered Las Vegas Boulevard until he found me. We never left one another's sight after that evening."

"You were married shortly after?"

"Yes." Selene's smile faded. "Do you understand, detective? I found him, the one. Can't you help me?"

"We were hoping you'd help us find him."

"If I knew..." Selene began to protest.

"We think you do. Where is he, Selene?"

"I don't know! How many times do I have to say it? We were with Gaelin as he played. Dean said something to Gaelin, Gaelin started acting weird and so did the dealer. They laid their cards down and... and..."

"Disappeared?"

"Yes." Selene dipped her head. "I know how it sounds, but if you just look at the security tapes, you'll see."

"What do you know about your husband?"

"That I am dead without him. That I am incomplete because I know he exists, incomplete because he has been ripped from my arms. He makes everything vile in this world perfect and he always will."

Detective Pinkerton stood and looked to the two way mirror on the adjacent wall.

"Dean is someone we have been looking for. We'd like to speak to him. We have a lot of questions to ask him." The detective approached the mirrored window with his hands clasped formally behind his back.

"Dean? You must be mistaken."

"How do you know?"

"Because I know my husband."

"You think you know your husband, but in truth you've only known him for a little over a month, correct?"

"Yes, but..."

"I hate to break it to you but Dean has a very dark past."

"You're lying."

"We've been looking for Dean for a very long time. He's a pretty nasty individual."

"Lies."

"Our pal Dean, your husband, had a very lucrative career as a bank robber in California. We had nothing on him until he screwed up in Los Angeles. Dean and his crew murdered twelve innocent people during a botched robbery."

"That doesn't make any sense. Dean isn't from Los Angeles."

"Dean didn't tell you he was from Los Angeles. He also didn't tell you that he was involved in the death of Sarah Gilbraunsen in 1998 during another botched bank robbery right here in Las Vegas. He disappeared, Selene, completely, until now."

"You're wrong."

"Well, that's what we're trying to sort out."

"The man I married is not a criminal, and he is certainly not a murderer. He only wants to love me and to write. Nothing else."

"Where did he work?"

"I don't know. He never went to work..." Selene's resolve began to fade.

"That's a little strange isn't it? Did he inherit some money from someone?"

"I don't know."

"Was he independently wealthy? Did you discuss a prenuptial agreement?"

"No. I don't know, please, I've told you everything, why aren't you trying to find my husband?"

"Dean O'Leary." Detective Pinkerton twisted the knife. "We'll find him, Selene. You can count on that. We'll also find out what you knew and when."

"Am I free to go?"

"I have some questions about…"

"Am I free to go?"

"Yes," the detective reluctantly replied. "But don't leave town, this isn't over." Detective Pinkerton left the interrogation room.

"She's lying," Stanley grunted as soon as the detective closed the door.

"Maybe. Chances are she doesn't know anything about Dean. Chances are, it's just another Irish kid with the same name as thousands of other Irish kids."

"Bullshit. This is it, Pinkerton, I can taste it. Dean fucked up and hit our radar again. He won't escape this time."

"We've got nothing to hold her on."

"I understand. Do you mind if I have a look at the security tapes?"

"Jesus, Stanley…"

"Thanks, I owe you."

Stanley and Pinkerton retreated to a small room with a large computer monitor and a single chair.

Pinkerton entered his passcode into the system and retrieved the digital security footage from Caesar's Palace.

Stanley stood expectantly over Pinkerton's shoulder. "Pretty fancy, Pinkerton. Do we have the overhead?"

"No. Technical difficulties before the event in question. Okay, here we are. There she is, calm, then... bam, she loses it."

"There are too many passing bodies blocking the view. Run it back ten, fifteen minutes," Stanley insisted impatiently.

The pair of street-tested eyes watched cards being flipped, waitresses coming and going, and the multicolored milieu of the addict.

"There!" Stanley shouted and pointed to a shadowy figure revealed only by a rapidly collapsing fissure in the crowd. "That's him."

"It isn't clear, that could be the person in the foreground reaching out their arm."

"You have to be kidding, Pinkerton; that's a person, standing next to Selene. You can nearly make out the outline of the player they are watching."

"Stanley, no offense, but you're reaching pretty hard on this."

"You're not reaching hard enough..."

"The story just doesn't check out. And besides..."

Stanley was gone. The room's door was sliding closed slowly.

"Don't do anything stupid, Stanley."

Selene blurred in a sea of hot steam. She bathed slowly, refusing to cry. Her hands reminded her of Dean. Her arms reminded her of Dean. The pleasure of the water's warmth reminded her...

How could he be a murderer? How could the man, who revealed to her the endless depths to which love can descend, be a monster? He couldn't. End of story. Selene, wrapped in terrycloth, slipped into their bed. Moonlight spread across their crumpled sheets. They had been here, just this morning. A beaten copy of *On the Road*, a half-pack of cigarettes, and a few typewritten pages of a letter cluttered his side table. She ran her fingers over the old paperback and re-read portions of the typed missive.

The sound of the stream is deafening. Who says you can't hear erosion? Your warmth has eroded the ice and stone I've so carefully built around my love. You claw at my defenses to reach inside, to feel connected, truly connected with me. You're saving me. I see forever in your eyes, and for once, I'm not afraid. It breathes fire into my veins. It inspires me.

Stanley pulled to a slow, deliberate stop across the street from Selene's address. The house was dark and the porch light was lit. Stanley waited; he had no choice. Pinkerton was useless, he wanted a closed case, and he couldn't see the big picture. O'Leary and his crew slaughtered twelve people in broad daylight on the corner of Sunset and Vine. Los Angeles went silent as every low-life informant and hustler was brought in. It was a parade of the seedy underbelly of Los Angeles. More than a few fish hit the net but LAPD never found a trace of the suspects. Stanley took it personally; with the vehemence of Ebola, he searched out and eliminated suspects. A young rookie working alongside Stanley turned up a homeless person who gave a description of a man from the movies. *You know, them old gangster movies. Suits and tommy guns...* Blah blah blah, or so it seemed at the time. Amateur footage confiscated from a tourist had shown a man in his early to mid twenties standing outside of the bank a few minutes before the crime was committed. It took the cooperation of seven departments, but Stanley found a State gaming license issued to a Dean O'Leary of Las Vegas, Nevada, with a pristine photograph, and a nice pre-millennial fingerprint. Stanley thought he had his man.

The detective had a point; Selene had only known Dean for a handful of weeks. The feeling of warmth and protection Dean enveloped her in was something she could never explain to the police. The moment she saw him, the way his hands moved was magic and his tired expression of joy reminded her of her childhood, of the innocence of human faith in things to come. She felt his presence immediately and still felt it now, he was not gone. Dean could have been many things before their eyes met, she may never know. All she could know is what they had shared, what transpired between them. The devotion they so properly succumbed to, the eternity they intended to spend in one another's embrace.

Stanley wanted to start in Las Vegas, but starting the investigation in Los Angeles, at the scene of the crime, ended up being the call of the day. By the time they were tipped off to Stretch, the crew's redneck driver, Dean was long lost in North Las Vegas. The police found his address by accident; he was careless one day and didn't wear a hat to the liquor store. He vanished, but the police found plenty of willing witnesses to his comings and goings. Then Dean disappeared for the final time. Stanley spent the better part of his career looking for him, but Stanley had neither the manpower nor the support from his Chief of Detectives to pursue O'Leary to the ends of the Earth. Now he had no restrictions and nothing to lose.

What was happening to her mind? How had Dean and Gaelin disappeared? It made less sense than Dean being a mass murderer. She twisted the steel band on her finger to remind herself that they were married, it really happened. She carelessly opened the drawer to Dean's side table. It was muddled with papers, pens, spare office supplies, and a black notebook. Selene had never seen him using the notebook. It was bound with a pair of rubber bands and looked like it had been through a particularly nasty neighborhood in Hades. Did she have the right to read it, now that he was gone? Now that she knew there was more to him than she could know? She numbly pulled at the first of two rubber bands, committing to the pain of knowing.

The lack of lights and the length of time he sat idly waiting were enough for Stanley. He'd never been good at stakeouts and now that he was off the job, the experience had only tarnished further. He walked slowly across the street and slid between two houses.

By way of two hip-high fences he approached Selene's backdoor. The two-story building left little room on either side, and Stanley had to be careful not to wake the neighbors. He removed tools from his jacket but the door popped open as soon as he applied pressure.

"Nice."

Stanley stood in the kitchen and let his eyes adjust to the dark house. He thumbed through a few bills on the kitchen counter and moved into the living room. The various drawers of the desk and of the large chest serving as a coffee table turned up rubbish and a few love letters. Stanley turned several times, looking for another place to search. His arm struck a small lamp near the sofa. He caught the lamp and froze.

Selene sat up in bed. What was that? She dropped the notebook on the floor and rushed to her closet. The house was silent. Selene fumbled for a baseball bat she'd kept near her bed, any bed, since high school and found it in the corner of the closet. The absence of noise pulsed, her blood rushed through her body. She stepped forward slowly, flattened against the wall, and moved toward the bedroom door.

Stanley took short careful steps toward a small antique file cabinet in an adjacent room. The room looked like an office and Stanley smiled, swimming in anticipation. He pulled gently on the top drawer and it creaked quietly.

Selene stopped. *Someone is in the office.* She walked to the doorway and turned her head slowly around the corner. A hunched man was running his fingers through Dean's file cabinet. Selene hoisted the baseball bat over her shoulder and rushed toward the man.

Stanley heard the faint click of the pine bat against the doorframe. His reaction was faster than he'd imagined possible at his age. He turned and fired his revolver at the shape about to overtake him. He fired twice more once the shape hit the ground. Stanley's hands shook and he dropped his weapon. Selene lay in a growing pool of crimson, lit by the midnight sun. As her life ebbed, the truth about Dean O'Leary slipped from Stanley's grip. Nothing discovered in the house would be admissible in court now; his obsession had been for naught.

He stayed until the inky night peeled into morning's light. There was nothing. The ramblings of a wannabe writer. Stanley's fear consumed him and he fled.

The notebook remained silent on the bedroom floor.

& Selene

Acknowledgements

Special thanks to: Nate Ragolia, Shaunn Grulkowski, and Spaceboy Books—I am incredibly grateful to them for keeping this manuscript alive. Kevin Staniec and Elise Portale, without whom this book would not be possible. William S. Burroughs, for changing my mind regarding the novel and inspiring a lifelong obsession.

& Selene

About the Author

William M. Brandon III is a dad and a husband. He sees coercive relationships as the root of oppression. From 2013 – 2021 William served as the Managing Editor for Black Hill Press and 1888. During his tenure he edited and curated *The Cost of Paper* series (*The Cost of Paper: Volume II, Volume III, Volume IV*), and edited *29 to 31* by Kevin Staniec, *The Pit and No Other Stories* by Jordan Rothacker, *Foster* by Scott Amstadt, and *A Little Evil* by B. Tanner Fogle.

About the Publishing Team

Nate Ragolia is a lifelong lover of science fiction and its power to imagine worlds more hopeful and inclusive than the real one. His first book, *There You Feel Free*, was published by 1888's Black Hill Press in 2015. Spaceboy Books reissued it in 2021. He's also the author of *The Retroactivist*, published by Spaceboy Books. He founded and edited *BONED*, a literary magazine, has created webcomics, and pets dogs.

Shaunn Grulkowski has been compared to Warren Ellis and Phillip K. Dick and was once described as what a baby conceived by Kurt Vonnegut and Margaret Atwood would turn out to be. He's at least the fifth best Slavic-Latino-American sci-fi writer in the Baltimore metro area. He's the author *Retcontinuum*, and the editor of *A Stalled Ox* and *The Goldfish* for 1888/Black Hill Press.

www.ingramcontent.com/pod-product-compliance
Lightning Source LLC
Chambersburg PA
CBHW061452210726
48287CB00007B/2467